# DAMAGED AND DIVERTING

*The (Sort of) End*

# MAPLE'S FANTASTIC STORIES

*Book Three*

## By the Mighty and Awesome Maple Twiggs

ISBN: 978-1-952065-05-7

First edition.

Maple Twiggs Publishing.

*Dedication: Type something emotionally touching here.*

# CONTENTS

# CHAPTER ONE.

*Not!ACat.*

*By Stella Grum.*

The walk to the clock tower was long, which was good because I got to stare at Archie the whole time—without him noticing. Have I mentioned that he's not *really* a cat? Have I mentioned that he's *actually* a super-attractive guy? I should probably mention that. Since it was the only thing going through my head.

Not!acat.

Not!acat.

Not!acat.

I stared at his back as he walked.

This guy was supposed to be my fated love?! I don't think so.

(Stella: Maple, Maple, Maple.

Maple: What? I'm trying to concentrate on my Very Important Farming Game right now. What do you need?

Stella: *Why'd you make Archie so attractive???* Normal-looking people—like me—don't end up with people that look like him. I think it's against the cosmic rules and divine order of the universe.

Maple: The male lead is supposed to be hot in these types of books.

Stella: But you didn't make *me* equally hot. So now it's unbalanced and weird.

Maple: I know. That makes it better.

Stella: *Hooowwwww???*

Maple: Because it makes you dreadfully uncomfortable. And I enjoy that immensely. Just wait until you find out what I do to you in Chapter Four. *It's the best thing ever.*

Stella: Um. Can I request that a different author write this third book?

Maple: Nope. I'm the only one weird enough to write these things.

Stella: Sigh. Well, that's true.)


We eventually made it to our destination. And without being accosted by Lontano, aka the psychotic skeleton in a bathrobe. So that was good.

The tower was home to a talking goose named George, who greeted us and invited us to sit down in his living room.

"Ah, the Jainkohiltzaile," the goose said upon my entry. "I guess Pitkin managed to accomplish his task."

"Pitkin?" asked Pu, the *actual* cat, currently sporting pink underwear on his head for Reasons.

"The robot in Archie's pocket," George replied. "He gave you the Game of Goose die that's in the Jainkohiltzaile's hand, which delivered you all here, right now."

Whoa. This goose knew everything. He was like a magical talking goose. Wait, he *was* a magical talking goose. Focus, Stella. Focus. Let's try to use your two remaining brain cells at once to stop thinking about not!acat Archie's pocket. Which was next to his not!acat body. His super attractive....

*What the heck was wrong with me?*

Not!acat Archie retrieved Pitkin the mustard tin robot from his jacket pocket and placed him on the coffee table. I set the Game of Goose die

3

next to him, and George placed a second die next to it.

"Clearly we're still missing something," George said and sighed. "One of you is going to have to call the game board pieces back here. Riot destroyed everything. Well, everything except my house. I've been trying to restore my board, but nothing's worked."

"I think that's going to have to be Stella," not! acat Archie said. "I don't have my full abilities at the moment. My powers became stronger once I returned to my Realm. But inside the game I don't know if they'll continue to strengthen or just stabilize."

"What's going on with you?" George asked.

"I'm sharing my powers with Tiziano, er, Lontano. Whatever he's calling himself now. And I've already accidentally brought him to locations I didn't want him to be. So if I cast very powerful spells I might bring him here, or the spells might not work at all."

"*Why are you sharing your powers with that idiot?!?*" George gasped.

"Uh, it was a sort of curse spell. He tried to steal my powers. It didn't entirely work."

"Ugh. Sylvie should've killed all those annoy-

4

ing gnats of death when she had the chance," George said. "Speaking of Sylvie, she's stuck inside a painting inside a room that you can only get to if you win the game."

"I knew about part of that situation," not!acat Archie said. "Win the game, though? Why do I feel like that's a trap?"

"Probably because it is one," Pu replied. "But what choice do we have except to try and win this thing?"

"Well, we'll have to deal with the trap when we get to it," not!acat Archie said. "Let's start with Stella's task."

"Wait, how am *I* supposed to get the game board pieces back?" I asked. "*I* don't know how to do anything."

The four of us took turns looking at each other for possible answers while Pitkin scratched his head.

"Well, when I was with the Four Dogs, Sylvie's caretakers, they used a fully-cast icon spell to call up Horografia. She was able to travel through time," not!acat Archie said. "Is there another type of icon spell Stella can cast in order to bring the game board pieces back?"

"So the Four Dogs can replicate the Godkiller's

spell capabilities?" Pu asked.

"Yes. But they're currently watching Lontano for me. So if I call them here, he may come along with them," not!acat Archie said, wincing.

"As much as I'd like to take a crap on that guy's head, none of us is a match for him right now. So we'd better keep him out of this for as long as possible," Pu said.

"We just need to find somebody else who knows about the Jainkohiltzaile's abilities, right?" George asked.

"And that would be? Who?" Pu asked.

"Linsenbardt," George said.

"Isn't that a kind of chocolate?" I asked.

"No. He's a kind of—well, he's a friend of mine. Library addict. All he does is read."

"We need practical knowledge here, George. Not book-smarts," Pu said.

"Sometimes you have to start at books," George said as he picked up the receiver of a fancy old-fashioned telephone. "Yeah, connect me with Linsenbardt, please. No, I don't know where he is right now. That's kind of your job as a magical phone. You track him down. Yeah, yeah. I know. Curse me out later, would you? Just find Linsenbardt. Yeah, Linsenbardt? Can you come on by? Yes. That's right."

Then George slammed the receiver onto the coffee table several times until a small, gold robotic worm fell out.

"I really hate traveling that way," the worm whined, then looked around at us with diamond eyes. "Now I'm gonna get a headache."

"Linsenbardt's a lejerdemani-crafted automaton silkworm," George explained, as I stared in bewildered amazement.

"Nice to meet you," Linsenbardt said as he wiggled toward Pitkin. "I love your rusty patina."

"Linsenbardt, we need to know about fully-cast icon spells of the Jainkohiltzaile," George said.

"Why would you need to know about those?"

"She needs to call my game board back here. Riot destroyed it, remember?" George asked. "But this Jainkohiltzaile's never been trained. So she's clueless."

"Ah. Riot. That weirdo. I suppose this would call for a Force of Virtue icon spell," Linsenbardt said, turning to me. "Ripa first cataloged those spells back in 1593. Most people don't know there are two levels to the spells. And humans don't even know they're spells. The first level is just basic lejerdemani magic. The second is for the Jainkohiltzaile and the Four Dogs. I ate a copy of the English edition back in the 1800s. So I should be able to remember what it said."

"You ate it?" I asked.

"Sometimes I can't stop myself from chewing on things. I'm sure it ended up in the House of Coventry, though. That's where all the really good stuff is. But Archie won't let me visit."

"That's because you'd probably try to eat an indestructible previously-destroyed book and break your jaw," George said.

"I can't say it wouldn't happen," Linsenbardt said.

"Wait, wait. Let's dial it back for a second," Pu interrupted. "Stella can barely wipe her own butt. How's she gonna fully-cast an icon? Icons don't just come when you call them."

Ah, Pu. Thank you for putting that image of me barely wiping my own butt into not!acat Archie's head. Thank. You. So. Much.

"I could probably fully-cast a Despair icon right now," I whispered.

"Apparently these types of spells come very naturally to Jainkohiltzailes," Linsenbardt explained. "I don't think we have anything to worry about."

Oh, really? Then why was I so damn worried?

# CHAPTER TWO.

*The Force of Virtue.*

*By Stella Octavius Grum.*

(Stella: Wait, is my middle name really Octavius???

Maple: No, not really. Although, that would make your initials SOG, which is really kind of funny.

Stella: Then *what is* my middle name?

Maple: Asswiper. That way your initials are SAG, which is what your tiny boobs will do when you are a thousand years old and decrepit.

Stella: Forget I asked.)

*Forza di Virtu.*
*'Tis a very handsome young Man, call'd*
*Bellerophon, mounted upon*
*Pegasus, who with a Dart kills a Chimera;*

*which allegorically signifies a*
*Certain multiform Variety of Vices, which*
*Bellerophon kills; the Etymology*
*Of his Name denotes a Killer of Vice.*

We assembled ourselves in a circle outside, near the red couch. Where I was supposed to call up an icon. Successfully.

Somehow.

"Bellerophon appears when the Force of Virtue spell is fully-cast. Just keep saying the words 'Forza di Virtu Bellerophon' over and over again as you visualize a handsome young man riding a Pegasus while he shoves a lance into a chimera," Linsenbardt explained from his perch on top of George's head. "Also, he's a killer of vices, so he'll only appear if the task you want him to accomplish is virtuous. So let's hope this is a righteous request."

"Why wouldn't it be?!" George huffed. "I have the *right* to have my game board back."

"So whiny," Linsenbardt replied.

Archie squatted down and demonstrated how I should hold my braceleted-hand over the ground where the game board should be. Like that would help somehow. George crossed his wings in front of himself, staring at me intently, while Pu just clicked his tongue repeatedly.

"There's a greater chance of butthole-shaped fairies flying out of my tiny pink butthole than this girl actually being able to call up a guy whose name she can't even pronounce," Pu said.

I glared at him. Then I squatted down next to Archie, and attempted to sort of say the words Linsenbardt had told me to repeat. Sort of.

Archie nodded reassuringly as if I had said them correctly. But I knew I hadn't. In fact, I could barely speak a word properly in front of him, never mind weird-sounding words like Belly-fun. And now everyone was staring at me, waiting for me to execute a spell that did something.

"Hold on a minute," I said as I stood up and gestured for Pu to follow me to the couch.

"You have to help me," I whispered to him.

"Help you? I'm not even your itzal izaki. I can't do a damn thing for you except, I don't know, produce nasty pukey-smelling hairballs for you every couple of months."

"But I really can't do this."

"Look at the bigger picture; you've been doing stuff all along. I may regard you as useless overall, but I admit you have done some stuff. Activating that Apollo. Listening to donkeys talk. Spinning turtle shells. Opening fountain-doors. Not to mention triggering the die that brought us here."

"Those were all by accident. Or just stupid little things. How could I possibly cast a spell that I can't even imagine what it is?"

"Is that the problem? You need to be able to visualize it fully before you do it? Linsenbardt just told you what to think about! Didn't you hear him?"

"I heard him. I did. I just. I can't. Archie's looking at me. I look so stupid."

"*Are you embarrassed right now? Really? What would be the point of that???* He already knows you're an idiot. And this isn't gym class, you moron. No one is looking at you, thinking about how much you suck at this, judging how baggy your clothes are, wondering about your bra size, or giggling at you flailing and almost drowning in the pool."

"I never. I didn't," I started to say something, mostly as an attempt to derail wherever this rant was going.

"The problem with you is you've spent your

whole life failing in your head before you've done a single thing," Pu continued. "You think of doing something, but simultaneously you think of failing at it. You never win in your own mind. So you never even try. You fail before you even begin. Self-doubt. Negative thoughts. The perpetual internal critic. That path will always lead to nowhere. 'I can't do it' your brain says. Of course you can't do it when you're permanently stuck in your own head."

"But…" I made my second, feeble attempt to turn this conversation in my emotional favor.

"In your mind you've failed at anything and everything you've ever done, ever thought of, ever tried even once," Pu ignored my 'but' and kept talking. "There's never been winning, victory, triumph. Not a single sense of accomplishment. There's only losing. The glass is always half-empty. Or more likely, just empty. No positives. No possibility of positives. No plus side. You've never done anything right in your whole life. *You have never done anything right.*"

I stared at Pu with wide teary eyes.

I guess this was the downside of asking for help from somebody who'd been living inside my head for the last ten or so years. It was like talking to my own miserable, self-loathing brain.

"But does that mean you should stop breathing?" Pu asked. "Stop living? Stop existing? Stop being? Does it? You don't have a choice. You are the Godkiller. So you must do something. This is the first step. The first moment. Forget about everything else. Just take this one step. Don't think about what comes next or what this means in the larger scheme of things. Don't think about whether Archie is looking at you. Just squat over there like you're about to take a poo. Without any dignity. With your hand above this muddy craphole-of-a-place, and say the damn words. That's the only thing you need to think about right now."

Pu jumped off the couch and pointed to my designated squatting place with the air of a perturbed military commander.

I complied with his instructions. While trying not to cry. As I made a profound mental note not to use him as a confidant in the future.

As I stared at the ground while in the pooing position, I thought about my father.

Stuck as a figurine. While I mentally struggled in this crappy situation.

Is this why he blocked my magic? Did he do it

to prevent me from making a fool of myself? Or to prevent some inevitable disaster I will cause? Did he automatically know I was going to suck at this?

Well, if I ever wanted a chance to see him again and ask those questions, I was going to have to start by making a fool of myself right here, right now.

I muttered 'Forza di Virtu Bellerophon' (or something like that) over and over again in an annoying loop, as I felt my bracelet get warmer and warmer. It was getting so hot I was pretty sure it was going to melt my wrist in half and my hand would just drop off. Eventually I couldn't tolerate the pain anymore.

"*Awssshpptt!!!* I think this thing is going to light me on fire!" I exclaimed as I quickly stood up and tried to yank the bracelet off my wrist.

A beam of light shot out of it, went straight up into the sky, and from that appeared the handsome young dude on his Pegasus, armed with aforementioned lance.

He was a real, full-size dude. In the flesh.

It had worked.

Somehow.

"*Ayyyyyyyeeeeeessshhhh,*" the handsome young

dude yelled as he jumped down from his winged horsie and shoved his lance into the ground. "Do you know what I was in the middle of just now?!?! *Do you even know?!?!*"

He looked at us all, apparently expecting an answer.

"Do you even *know* what you just interrupted so that I can do whatever *asinine* thing you're gonna ask me to do?" he continued. "*Do you even know?!?*"

"Is this a trick question?" Pu asked.

"What the heck's on your head?" Belly-fun asked. "Oh, never mind. I was just talking to Fortezza! Girl's never given me the time of day before and I've been asking her out for years. This was the first bloody time she even acknowledged my existence! And yet, here I am. Here. I. Am. I mean what the heck is so important? Have you seen her? Have you seen her? I mean, I'm talking about Fortezza here. *Fortezza.* So get on with it. What do you want?"

"Ummmm," I non-answered, since he was now staring me down.

"She needs the game board pieces that used to exist in this place," Archie interjected, saving me from looking more stupid than I already looked.

"*Game board pieces?!* You guys get weirder and weirder every time you call me," the handsome young dude replied, as he retrieved his lance and jumped back on his Pegasus.

Then he flew into the air and started to recite something I couldn't understand as he held his lance above his head and circled above us.

"Ancient Greek," Pu said to me, explaining why I couldn't understand this dude. "Curse words mostly."

I watched Bellerophon intently and prayed that Pegasus wouldn't poop on us as he flew in a circle above our heads.

Wait, was Pegasus a boy horsie or a girl horsie?

Oh well, that's not really important.

I guess if I looked more closely, I could tell....

Then the ground started to shake and crack open, and it was difficult to remain standing. The four of us ran to the couch and planted ourselves on it. For safety. As if being on a couch would help. Somehow.

Huge tiles floated up out of the cracks and then the ground re-sealed itself. The tiles assembled into a pattern in the air above our heads like a massive alien spaceship. Then they started glowing very brightly, disappeared, and re-appeared underneath our feet as a giant game board that continued off in all directions as far as the eye could see.

*"This thing is massive!!!* How many spaces are on this thing???" Pu asked, shocked.

"63," George answered.

"Seems to be a lot more than 63 spaces here," Pu mumbled. "Why'd this thing have to be so big? Did the creator have a Napoleon complex or something?"

"The scale is for dramatic effect, you peasant," George replied.

*"Peasant?!!?? What?!?!"* Pu yelled, grabbing for George.

I dragged Pu off the couch before a fistfight could start.

Once the game board pieces stopped glowing, all of the burnt stumps were revived into a low, lush hedge that bordered both sides of the game board spaces. Large white eggs began to sprout from the bushes like extremely fast-growing fruit.

*"Is that it?!?!"* Bellerophon called down to us, still angry.

"For now!!!" Pu shouted.

Bellerophon scowled as the beam of light once

again appeared from my bracelet, and sucked him and his horsie back in.

"Where did he come from?" I asked. "And where did he just go?"

"God, don't start on that nonsense. He came from the Realm of Magic. One of the Eight Realms. Where all of the Icons live," Pu answered.

"What are the other seven Realms?" I asked.

"There's the Realm of the Present. That's Earth where you came from," Pu replied. "Realm of the Dead, self-explanatory. Realm of the Gods. Realm of the Itzal Izaki. Realm of Destruction. Where we currently find ourselves, sort of. This game seems to be in a weird offshoot dimension of that, the House of Coventry."

"That's only six realms," I said, repeating them in my head and counting on my fingers.

"The other two are secret," Pu answered, crossing his arms.

"You're joking, right?" I asked.

"Nope. I'll tell you about them when you've earned the right to learn about them. So far you've proven yourself to be 99.9% worthless. So you can't learn about them yet."

I looked at Archie.

He shrugged.

I wondered if one of the two secret Realms was like the Realm of Candy and Desserts where everything was edible. That would be nice. Hopefully itzal izaki aren't allowed to go there.

"Well, roll the damn dice, you silly woman," Pu said, pointing at me, the silly woman with the damn dice.

"Wait, stuff keeps happening without me knowing what's about to happen. Before I roll the dice, *what's going to happen?* Explain it to me in small words," I said.

"Yes, well. Good point. I'll try to do that," Archie agreed, while Pu moaned with impatience. "The board has a spiral shape, like the Fibonacci spiral of a Nautilus shell. You begin at one end, and you can only finish the game if someone lands exactly on the 63rd space at the center of the spiral."

"So we take turns rolling these dice, moving ahead on the board until someone lands on 63?" Pu asked. "That sounds like the lamest game in the history of the universe."

"*Lame?!?!*" George yelled.

"No, no. Well, yes," Archie replied. "Hold on, let me finish explaining. We take turns rolling

21

the dice. There are spaces like go back to the beginning, or roll again, or switch places with another player. And there are other locations that we're sent to besides this place. For each game we have to go to at least three of those or the dice won't let us win. At those places we'll have tasks to complete in order to move forward in the game."

"That's lame. *And* dumb," Pu said.

"You're dumb," George responded. "It's a wonderful game!"

"No, it's stupid. What moron invented it?" Pu asked.

"No one knows," Linsenbardt said.

"Even I don't know. And I've only ever lived here, probably for thousands of years. I don't really keep track of time, though," George said.

"Sylvie thought it was Old Kunkerpot who made it, the Jainkohiltzaile before her," Archie said. "But I think it was made by a God of Destruction long before my time. I'm not sure though. The game is constantly changing and updating the locations within itself. So it's sort of like a living, thinking being."

"That's way creepy," Pu said. "Like—*way*."

I'm glad I wasn't the only one discomforted by

that explanation.

"That's just how it is," George said and sighed. "Try not to think about it too much with your tiny cat brain."

"If you don't stop insulting me, I'm gonna have thousand-year-old-goose *foie gras* for dinner tonight," Pu said.

"Why you insolent little…" George began.

"Stella, roll the dice before these two kill each other," Archie whispered to me.

"But if I roll them, we have no idea what'll happen, right?" I whispered back. "We don't know where we'll end up? Is that what you're saying? Because that's what I'm hearing."

"Yes, that's basically true," Archie said.

"So we could end up in a pit full of boiling oil and boiling snakes?" I asked.

"Hopefully not," Archie said, frowning. "That's not the type of game this is. I mean, I don't know what Riot did to it though…."

"Lovely," I said and sighed. "Just great."

"You can roll the damn dice or we can stand around waiting until that crazy operatic clown figures out how to get in here," Pu interjected. "And if he captures you, he may or may not be able to kill you. But he can at least torture you for a thousand years until you're finally capable of dying. So what'll it be, Fatty?"

"Ummm," Archie said as he held up one hand in an attempt to stop Pu's happy train of happy thoughts.

"Fine," I said as I threw the dice at Pu. I mean, I threw them up into the air sort of in Pu's direction in order to roll them. "Today's as good a day as any to end up in a pit full of boiling oil and boiling snakes."

The dice soared into the air and landed with some bouncing 'plinks' onto the game board, as George the Magical Goose of Magic looked down at them.

"Well, enjoy your time at The Prison, where you just landed after rolling a lovely sixteen, double eights! Lucky! We'll see you again when you're done with your prison-related task," he said.

"*The what?!?!*" I tried to ask, but instead of answering me George opened up his wings and a warm, bright light emanated from them and enveloped us, blinding us in the process. Or at least I was blinded. Maybe the cat, the god, and the caterpillar could see just fine.

The light faded and faded and faded, until we

were in complete darkness.

# CHAPTER THREE.

*Meanwhile, with the Crazy Operatic Clown.*

*As Presented by Morrow Demington.*

"*What just happened?!?!?*" the handsome young man in his bathrobe, who had just been a skeleton, screamed at us after Archie, Pu, Stella, and her sofa disappeared from the courtyard.

In his anger he was feverishly pacing back and forth, his bathrobe beginning to fall off.

"The MacGuffin," Nora whispered to Ellie and me, pointing at him.

"Sssssshhhh," I responded. "That must be Tiziano."

Meanwhile, Ellie could not take her eyes off this weirdo.

"I love you!" she called out to him, already

26

head over heels.

Her infatuation with Archie was apparently only in effect as long as he was next to her.

"Of course," the man answered. "Wait, who are you people?"

"This is the part where we do something pro-active," I whispered to my sisters.

Nora winked at me, grabbed my hand, and I grabbed Ellie's. Then she announced: "We're rubber, you're glue. Whatever spell you throw at us bounces right off, and sticks to you."

"What?" he asked. "What was that? Ugh, I don't have time for this. Do you know where those morons just went to?"

"No," I answered.

"Somewhere other than here," Nora added, in a very helpful manner.

"Fine, fine. Be brats," he said as he tried to cast his signature paralysis spell on us, but it went right back onto him.

A look of pure terror crossed his face, but it quickly transformed into anger.

"*Who are you people?!*" he asked again.

"Can you move?" Nora asked.

"I think you already know the answer to that," he said.

"Do you think it's okay if I touch him?" Ellie whispered.

"Noooooooooo," I replied.

With some effort, he broke his own paralysis spell. Which is kind of the downside of this type of magic. If you're powerful enough to cast such a spell, you're probably powerful enough to break such a spell.

Then he cast the type of transformation spell he had used to turn Penny and Derek into porcelain figurines. Only this time he was too angry to choke us and sing opera as he did that, so he just glared at us as he spat out Italian curses under his breath.

Unfortunately, or fortunately—depending on your point of view—he just managed to turn himself into a porcelain figurine of a young woman wearing a big straw hat and carrying a pile of vegetables in her apron.

The string of Italian curse words continued after he had transformed himself back into a man. But unfortunately, or fortunately—depending on your point of view—he was still in the woman's dress, hat and apron, with vegetables. Which he proceeded to throw violently onto the floor.

"*What are you vile things?!?!*" he screamed as he ripped the hat off, clawed at the dress, and stomped on the tomatoes and artichokes.

He then threw a fireball at us with a rather strong conflagration spell.

It quickly bounced right off, not even leaving a mark. But it completely engulfed him.

"He's not really thinking this through, is he?" I asked.

"I don't know why Eagle said we couldn't handle this guy," Nora said. "We're doing fine. This isn't exactly the epic 'to-the-death' battle I expected to have with him."

"Yeah, but we can't stand here for the rest of our lives," Ellie said. "This is what you'd call a stalemate. Until he figures out a way to defeat us."

Tiziano broke his own conflagration spell. But he was still nearly burnt into a crispy critter. He was now covered in black soot. His peasant girl dress was mostly destroyed. And any skin I could see was definitely burnt and blistering.

"Well, that sucked on levels that are difficult to describe," he said as he cast a restoration spell on himself, reverting to the attractive un-burnt man, in his bathrobe.

And then he sat down on the remaining red sofa.

"Cry over spilled milk," Nora said, casting another spell.

Tiziano started sobbing like a toddler who had just run out of cookies, while holding his head in his hands. I looked at Nora with confusion.

"What?" she asked. "If he's busy crying like a baby, then he can't think about how to defeat us."

"Good idea," Ellie said. "But couldn't you have made it a spell where he's distracted by stripping himself instead?"

"This isn't that kind of book, Ellie," I said and sighed.

"Are you sure? We could make it that kind of book," she replied, adding a flirty tone to her voice.

A dog entered the courtyard, walking like a human. He glared at Tiziano. And then three more dogs joined him.

"I'm not sure what's going on here, but where did the new Jainkohiltzaile and Archie go?" the first dog asked.

"We have no idea," Ellie answered.

"*Uggghhh*," the smallest dog said. "That's it. I

resign myself to death by chocolate. I'm going to the kitchen and eating my weight in choco bars. Nobody stop me!"

"Stop you? I'll join you," the first dog replied.

"What should we do now?" the furriest dog asked.

"The loosened lug nut is loose," the fourth dog announced.

Tiziano stood up and screamed, partially in his attempt to break the crying spell and partially out of obvious frustration. He began to swear in Italian while punching the sofa, repeatedly.

And then we were no longer in the courtyard.

We were in a different place, outside, surrounded by a low hedge maze with eggs growing all over it. Under our feet was a beautiful marble sidewalk that had numbers and images carved into it.

Tiziano continued to punch the sofa and swear —in between sobs—unaware of what had just happened.

I looked around for those four dogs, but they were nowhere to be found.

It was just this psychopath and us.

"What just happened?" I asked.

"You've entered the Game of Goose," a white goose said as he came around the hedge corner and frowned at us. "But I'm not sure how you did that. My name is George. Who are you people?"

"Nora, Morrow, Ellie, and Tiziano," Nora announced, pointing to everyone as she listed our names.

"Lontano!!!" Tiziano screamed as he stopped punching the sofa. "My name is Lontano now! I am the God of Destruction!"

"Sure you are, buddy. And I'm the God of Flatulence. Nice to meet you," George said. "I'd love to call you the God of Destruction, but you don't look anything like Archie. So try again, smartie."

Lontano—I guess that's his name now—looked like he wanted to dropkick the goose. But he was still under Nora's crying spell, so instead he just wept more.

"What's with this guy?" George asked us.

"He's dealing with some stuff right now," I answered.

"Yeah, like being defeated by three little girls," Nora added.

"Why are we here?" Ellie asked George. "We were just in the Realm of Destruction. Archie, Stella, and Pu disappeared. And then we showed up here. Do you know what's going on?"

"Ahhhh. Tiziano. *That* Tiziano. The one who tried to steal Archie's powers. I get it now. You four seem to have followed Archie into the Game of Goose because Titty-tano there is bonded with him."

"My. (sob) Name. (sob) Is. (sob) Not. (sob) Titty-tano," Lontano cried.

"So what do we do now?" Ellie asked. "Is Archie here?"

"No, he's playing the game. They went to The Prison," George answered. "But once they're done they'll come back here to roll again."

"Do we play the game, too, then? In order to join them?" Nora asked. "Or do we just wait here until they return?"

"If I were you I'd wait until they come back. Makes it all less complicated," George explained. "Although, I don't really understand who you three girls are...."

But his sentence was cut off. By the fact that the four of us were no longer with George the Goose. Instead we were standing in the woods on a dirt path.

In front of us was a rock outcropping that looked like it was melting. Water dripped down the rock wall, flowed over the melting part, and gathered on a string of objects that hung across the wall. Shoes. Gloves. A lobster. A teakettle. A sock. A cricket bat. And dozens of teddy bears hung from ropes, slowly being petrified by the mineral-rich water. About half of the objects had 'turned' into stone. It was one of the weirder things I have seen in my short life.

"Those are disconcerting," Ellie announced, pointing to the bizarre objects.

"Well, where are we now?" I asked. "I'm gonna get motion sick if we keep bouncing around like this."

"You're at Mother Shipton's Petrifying Well," a teddy bear answered. "Well, not the real thing. That's on Earth. You're inside a map that was once painted on a bulletin board at the entrance to the park in Knaresborough."

"Okay, those things are *extremely* disconcerting," Ellie said, clearly terrified of the talking bear.

"We're in the stupid Game of Goose!" Lontano screamed, in between curses and sobs.

"Oooh, yippee!!!" Nora squealed as she started clapping.

Oooh, no.

# CHAPTER FOUR.

*The Prison of Awkwardness.*

*By Stella.*

I stumbled forward in the pitch-blackness and touched a wet, slimy, cold stone wall.

"Ewwwwww," I said.

"*Watch out for rats*," Pu whispered.

"*No, please, not rats!*" I panic-whispered back.

"There aren't rats in the game's prisons," Archie said. "I mean, usually. Unless they happen to be in the original artwork."

"*Riiiiiggghhhttt*," Pu mocked him.

"The original artwork?" I asked. Confused.

"Each Game of Goose location is inside a destroyed work of art, or image of some sort, like a map or picture, which was originally created by a lejerdemani," Archie said.

"While we all ponder the pointlessness of that

aspect, can someone shed some light on this occasion?" Pu asked.

A light appeared in Archie's hand.

It was a small flashlight.

From his pocket.

"You're a god," Pu said. "You can't even create a fireball in your hand? Or just like snap your fingers and light the room?"

"Why should I do that when I have a flashlight?" Archie asked.

"Why do I end up feeling like the stupid one every time I ask you a question?" Pu asked.

"Plus, I like flashlights," Archie said. Then he lit his face from below like a serial killer and smiled.

"Ugh, don't do that. Then you look scary," I said.

"I do?" he asked.

"Well, scary—but not ugly," I said. "You'd never look ugly."

"Oh," Archie said.

"Are you two *flirting*?" Pu asked, mischievously.

"No," I answered.

I was *not* flirting.

I. Swear.

Something started scratching on the wall like nails on a chalkboard and a chill ran up my spine.

"*Ohmygod, is that a rat???*" I whisper-gasped.

A small fireball appeared in Pu's paw, and he threw it at the ceiling. It stuck like a spitball, and began to grow and spread, lighting the whole windowless prison cell we were now in.

"No, *it's not a rat*, you nimrod. It was me. Even if the *god* can't cast a spell to light a room, I can," Pu said.

"I could've done that if I wanted to," Archie replied.

In the newly lit room I noticed some wooden benches near the wall, so I sat down. Even if they were covered in gross stuff, I was lazy and tired of standing.

"Speaking of flirting," Pu said as he sucked his teeth, annoyingly, and jumped up on the bench to sit next to me.

"We weren't speaking of that," I said.

"*Speaking of flirting*," Pu angrily repeated. "I just realized something. For two people who are supposed to fall in love, you guys *really* suck at the romantic tension stuff."

"We're not going to fall in love," I said, shaking my head. "That's just stupid stuff the dumb author suggested. But it's not going to happen."

I half-glanced at Archie. He was busy, working hard, staring at the wall.

"How do you know it's not going to happen?" Pu asked.

"It can't happen," I whispered. "He's, like, a man. I mean, a lot older than me. Look at him. He's like in college."

I rubbed my forehead. Archie politely coughed, I guess as a sign that he was agreeing with me.

Pu looked back and forth between Archie and me for several minutes.

"*College?* Really?" he eventually said. "You're so stupid. He's a god. You're a Godkiller. Age doesn't matter. You're outside the framework of normal Earthly lives."

I politely coughed this time.

"Well, she's right though. I am older than her," Archie said. "Falling in love would be a bit weird."

"See? Even he said it'd be weird," I confirmed, my heart sinking a little bit.

"*Weird?* When is falling in love not weird?" Pu asked. "You two are supposed to fall in love. And that's that. Euripides once wrote that whoever yields properly to fate is deemed wise among men, and knows the laws of heaven."

"Well, I'm definitely not a wise man. I'm not even a man," I said, adding a fake-chortle at the end.

"You dodo bird. I'm pretty sure you have no idea what I just tried to tell you," Pu said as he rolled his eyes.

"Alright, I admit I was never very good in English class or the Classics or Latin, or whatever class Euripeedes would be covered in," I said.

"Should I say it to you in the original Greek? *Would that help?*" Pu inquired sarcastically. "Fate. Moíra. Patu. Destino. Unmei."

"That didn't help me at all," I replied.

"Wait. I have a better idea!" he exclaimed as he climbed up into my lap, and put his paws on my cheeks.

His mood had gone from annoyed to instantly euphoric. I had no clue why.

"*Ero maitasuna ukitu bat*, a touch of mad love," he said.

Then he grinned at me mischievously and I felt a surge of fizzy power transfer from him and warm my cheeks.

"What'd you just do???" Archie asked, stepping

toward us. "*Did you just make her fall in love with you???*"

*He did what???*

"I did no such thing," Pu replied.

"What *did* you do then?" Archie asked.

"Well—well, you'll find out when you find out," Pu said, shrugging but still smiling like a crazed moron.

What did he do? And why was he so happy about it?

"God, my face is on fire," I said as I realized that my warmed cheeks were still quite warm and getting warmer.

Did he cast a spell to melt my face off???

"Are you okay?" Archie asked as he reached toward my cheeks where Pu had put his paws.

"*Aaaaand* you'll find out sooner than I thought you would," Pu said.

Then he tilted his head and tried not to laugh.

As Archie's fingertips lightly touched my cheeks I blacked out.

I probably passed out and flopped onto the ground. And laid there, drooling like an idiot. That's my guess.

Let's hope I didn't wee myself.

# CHAPTER FIVE.

*After I Touched Stella's Cheeks.*

*Um, Face Cheeks.*

*As Presented By Archie.*

Yes, it's me again. Archie.

Stella doesn't quite remember what happened next, so I'm going to have to write this part. She didn't pass out, though. So don't worry about that. She was quite awake and…active.

As I touched her face she started laughing hysterically.

"*God, you're really good-looking!* Has anyone ever told you that you're super-super handsome?" she asked. "Like you look funny, but it's a good funny."

Then she pressed my hands against her face as she looked up at me, smiling.

"What are you doing?" I asked.

"Right now? Wondering how soft and cuddly you are," she said.

"What?"

"*What?*" she repeated in a fake deep voice.

"Was that supposed to be my voice? What's she doing?" I asked Pu.

"She's acting like the crazy smitten loon she really is, deep down inside her soul," he said and then grinned.

"*What* did you do to her???" I asked.

"Yeah, *wha*t did you do to her? I mean, me. What's wrong with me?" Stella asked. "I can't stop looking at this guy. He's so cute it's giving me goosebumps. But not like the bad goosebumps that make you want to pee. The good ones that make you feel alive."

"Oh uh," I said, unsure of how to respond to that.

"Are you ticklish?" she asked as she wiggled her fingers at me.

"No," I lied, but I started giggling. And then she started giggling.

*Why did I have to be ticklish?*

Why was I acting like a teenage boy?!?!?

*Was Pu's spell having an effect on me, too?*

She began to walk her fingers in the air toward

me while grinning.

"Pu, explain. What kind of spell did you cast?" I asked.

"It's a unique and peculiar kind of spell. Every time she touches a man, she'll act unique and peculiar," he said and laughed.

"Peculiar? Like how?" I asked, as Stella winked at me.

"She'll become a madly-in-love weirdo," he replied.

"So it's a love spell. But wait, any man? If *any man* touches her?" I asked.

"Any man. Well, probably," Pu said. "It wasn't specific to you. You're just the only man here."

"And she'll act madly-in-love with *any man* that touches her?" I asked.

"Oh, yes. I see the problem now that you mention it," Pu said as he tapped his chin. "Well anyway, if it's *any man* this will be more entertaining for me. Which is really the only thing that matters."

Stella had started to hold my hands while pushing back my cuticles on my fingernails. Like a bizarre, impromptu manicure. Um.

"Turn it off," I ordered Pu. "Take the spell away."

"Nope, I can't," he replied, shaking his head.

"Why not? You put it on her. You take it off her."

"Nope. I made it so she's the only one who can un-cast the spell from herself."

Pu smiled from ear to ear.

"What? *How'd you even do that?* That's insane!" I said.

"No, no. Not in-sane. In-spired, my friend. *In-spired*. And an itzal izaki specialty."

"Stella, Stella. Concentrate," I said as I looked into her eyes. "Un-cast the spell from yourself. Can you do that?"

"How would I possibly know how to do that?" she asked after she blinked at me a few times.

Then she stood up and grabbed me in a very tight hug that nearly squeezed the air out of my lungs.

"You can teach me how though," she said.

"I don't know how he did it. Pu, you show her how to do it," I said, while staring at her, her face now inches from mine.

"Hmmm. The spell will un-cast itself when it's no longer needed. How about that for an explanation?" Pu asked.

What an annoying cat. Well, I can't blame him.

That's just how itzal izaki are.

I kept staring down into Stella's eyes. Thinking about how to break this spell. Thinking about how nice it felt to be hugged. No, wait. Ssshhh. Pretend I didn't write that last part.

Yes, I've had people hug me before. People often throw themselves at me. I don't mean that as bragging. Unfortunately, it's one of the side effects of being the God of Destruction. People are drawn to me, except for a few here and there, who have other things on their minds. For example, Sylvie had Ozzie on her mind from the first time I met her. So she never showed any interest in me.

Honestly, I'm not that interested in people. Probably because they keep throwing themselves at me. I'm not really sure whose idea of a joke that is.

But Stella's so odd, unexpected. And totally adorable. No. I shouldn't have feelings for this girl. She's just a girl. But, well—there *was* something attractive about someone being weirdly flirtatious without even caring how it made her look. I guess it was because of the spell. She didn't know what she was doing.

Usually people put on such a fake show to attract me, acting the way they think I want them to act. Cool, sexy, demure, aloof. Meanwhile, Stella had started smelling my chest through my shirt.

"What *is* she doing?" I asked.

"Clearly, she's smelling you. Go on, hold her," Pu said and then he made a kissy face and winked, as if he knew what had been going through my mind for the past few minutes.

"Yeah, go on, *hold her*," Stella agreed, tightening her hug, although I don't know how her grip could get any tighter.

It was getting difficult to breathe and my vision began to blur. Was it possible to pass out from lack of oxygen from a hug?

"We can't go on like this," I said as I looked at Pu with pleading eyes. "How are we supposed to play the game if she's like this? Please help me take this spell off of her."

"Fate. Moíra. Patu. Destino. Unmei," Pu repeated, smirking the whole time. "'The nobly born must nobly meet his fate.'"

"Euripides, again. Thank you," I said and sighed.

"I don't care if you're in college," Stella said into my chest. "I'll still be with you even if you're old. If you want to be with me. I mean, I'm emotionally unstable and immature right now, but I doubt that'll change in the future. So it's not like me aging a few more years will help in that regard."

"It's not a matter of a few more years," I said. "There's a lot, *lot more* than a few years standing between us."

"What are you guys doing in here?" a man asked from the other side of the door.

"I'm running love experiments!" Pu called to him, happily.

"Archie, why do you have a girl attached to your chest?" Leonardo da Vinci asked as he walked into the cell after unlocking the door.

"Thank goodness you showed up, Leo! I was about to bust down this door with a wicked awesome door busting spell," Pu said. "Now turn around. You and I are gonna leave the cell, and lock Stella and Archie in it. If we leave them here for two to three days that should be enough time."

"Enough time for what?" Leonardo asked.

"Stuff to happen," Pu answered.

"Stuff? Hmmm. Well, I'm not sure Archie is going to do 'stuff' even with two or three or seventeen days. Can't you see the look on his face because that girl's hugging him? I think his brain is starting to malfunction. Human affection does nothing for him."

"Human affection does nothing for *me*, but I'm a cat and humans disgust me. Surely this guy with his guy brain and his guy body chemistry can give in to human affection?" Pu asked.

"Probably not. It bores him. Wait, you're Pu. So where's Derek?" Leonardo asked.

"We won't discuss where he is. Because if we do, my murderous feelings for a certain idiot will return, and I'll want to hunt him down and drown him in a giant jar of raspberry marmalade."

"How do you know Pu?" I asked.

"I taught some adjunct lejerdemani classes a while back and Derek was in them. Good guy," he said.

"That suckerfish on Archie's chest is his daughter and the next Godkiller," Pu said.

"Really? He had a daughter? I thought his wife couldn't carry children," Leonardo said.

"She couldn't," Pu said.

"So where did I come from?" Stella asked.

"You don't want to know," Pu said. "Well, anyway. Archie, Stella, have a good time here for a few days."

And with that he tried to drag Leonardo out of the cell by his ankle.

"You can't leave us in here," I said and sighed. "We've got to play the game, remember?"

"I think they could leave us in here for a few hours," Stella suggested. "I want to count your eyelash hairs. They're so pretty."

I....

"Well, Leo—can we leave them alone in here for a few hours, and then do the dumb game task?" Pu asked. "Or can the dumb game task be opening the dumb prison cell door? If so, that's accomplished. Check. So now you and I can go have some macchiato while Stella counts stuff."

"No, just unlocking the door isn't enough," I replied.

"Wait," Leonardo interrupted. "Let me do this the right way."

He left the cell, locked the door, unlocked the door, walked back into the cell, and said: "Welcome to my prison. I'm Leonardo da Vinci. Well, I'm dead. So I'm the ghost of Leonardo da Vinci. But don't worry, I'm still Leonardo da Vinci. Pause for dramatic effect. Pause. Pause. Do you guys think that pause was long enough?"

"Ah. That's good old Leo. Nuttier than a rabid squirrel in a nut factory where all the nuts are laced with mercury," Pu said. "Was that it? Was that all that needed to happen? Can we leave these two alone now?"

"No, I'm supposed to give you a task. Once it's completed I give you a prize, and then you can leave," Leonardo explained. "But if you want to trap these two together I have a much better room for that than this cell."

"I'm intrigued," Pu said and smiled.

"Can we just hear about the task?" I asked.

"No, I'm intrigued, too," Stella interrupted. "What kind of room are we talking about?"

Then her stomach rumbled in angry hunger.

"Ahhh, but there's that," she said and sighed. "I feel really lightheaded, you guys."

She stopped hugging me, sat down on the bench, and closed her eyes, resting her head in her hands.

"When did you eat last?" I asked.

"I don't know. When did we eat? You were a cat then," she said. "A cat! Ahaha. Hmmm. Um. Wait, what just happened? Where'd this old guy come from?"

"You don't remember Leonardo coming into the cell?" I asked.

"No. And why does your tuxedo jacket look so disheveled?" she asked me.

"Dammit!" Pu said. "I think my spell wore off because she's hungry! *What the heck?!*"

"Come, let's retire to my chambers where you can get some food, get rested, and we can discuss your task," Leonardo said.

# CHAPTER SIX.

*In Which Archie Eats a Lot of Jam Pastries.*

*By Stella.*

I had a vague idea of the things that had happened in the prison cell, but it seemed like a very confusing dream. Had I blacked out? Or had I been awake? I couldn't quite put the pieces together. So I decided it was best not to ask anyone for specifics. Clearly Pu had cast a spell on me, but it had worn off. So I'll just pretend nothing happened. Yes. That's a perfect solution. Yes. Right?

"Don't touch me. Or any man," Archie whispered to me as we paraded out of the prison cell, following this old man Leonardo down a pitch-black hallway.

I wanted to stop and think about that perplexing directive, but being in a really scary-looking prison was kind of absorbing my attention. We had managed to land ourselves in a place that was somehow even more distracting than Archie.

We turned a corner and walked into a cavernous space several stories high, where dozens of stone staircases rose into a shadowy mist that was thicker in the corners and edges of the huge hall. Three stone towers with balconies sat in the corners of the space to observe what happened below. The only light I could see came from high above. Chains, shackles, and torture tools hung from the walls. Strange machines sat near the towers. This was apparently a dungeon, but it literally looked like a black and white drawing. I felt like I was inside a textbook illustration. Nothing looked real.

"Giovanni Battisti Piranesi's *Le Carceri d'Invenzione*," Leonardo said, looking at me. "I live inside Piranesi's prints. Those that have been destroyed and exist here in the House of Coventry. He was also a lejerdemani."

I acknowledged this information with a blank look, nodding at him, but understanding nothing.

"My home is a three-dimensional rendering of

Piranesi's images of the prisons of the imagination," he continued. "They're a series of underground vaults, a labyrinth really, with all sorts of engines and machinery, wheels, cables, pulleys, levers, catapults. Everything I need for my work."

"I bet this place is awesome for echoing curse words. *Bollocksssss!!!!*" Pu yelled.

The word echoed against the walls, and rang in my ears for what seemed like several minutes.

"I see…" I said and nodded again.

"Well, besides the echoing thing, the best part is that I'm completely and utterly alone," Leonardo said and smiled.

I looked back at him and half-smiled.

People don't usually imprison themselves, right? That's weird, right?

Why did he want to be alone?

"I get so much more done now that I'm dead. And here in *le carceri* no one bugs me! And well, most people don't know where I am. So don't tell anybody," he said as he placed his finger to his mouth and winked.

"I don't think anybody would want to come here willingly," I answered, as we walked by a man who was tied to a carved column. Another guy cranked a lever and pulley machine that stretched his legs.

"Hey, whassup beautiful?" the victim asked me as we shuffled by him.

"Don't touch him," Archie said, sliding between me and said victim.

Why would I even do that?

"Shouldn't he be screaming?" I asked.

"Nah, it's mostly just for show," Leonardo answered.

We made our way up staircases, across drawbridges, and along balconies to Leonardo's main living space—several rooms taken right out of an English country cottage with endless flowery cupboards, cushions, and couches.

Leonardo served us a Victorian high tea 'with all of the extras,' but minus meats because he's a veggie. I didn't know what I was eating or drinking. I just knew I was hungry. About halfway through our meal, I began to hope and pray that Piranesi had etched out some modern bathrooms, with flushing toilets and running water.

"Oh, don't worry. I had all of that installed when I moved in," Leonardo said to me, smiling.

Wait, was this guy reading my mind?

Had he been doing that all along?

*Who was this guy?*

"I'm the ghost of Leonardo da Vinci," he said. "And yes, I've been trained to have that particular skill."

What did he mean? Leonardo da Vinci?

Like—*the* Leonardo da Vinci?

The guy who painted the Sixteenth Chapel ceiling or something?

"I'll pretend you didn't think that last part," he said. "Yes. *The* Leonardo da Vinci. You missed my main intro because you were attached to Archie at the time."

He could totally read my mind.

He continued smiling at me as he poured me more Darjeeling.

I tried to clear my mind of stuff I didn't want him to know. Which promptly made me think of all the stuff I didn't want someone to know. What did he mean attached to Archie? What was I doing to Archie?

Archie....

"I agree. He does have lovely, muscular shoulders," Leonardo said, nodding. "I've always thought so. And just *beautiful* eyes. If I was 525 years younger, I mean, well...."

He looked at Archie, who was lovingly shoving a jam-covered crumpet into his face in one mouthful. Despite how elegant and refined he looked in his tuxedo, he was clearly uninhibited when it came to pastries.

"He does have a soft spot for sweet things," Leonardo said as he winked at me.

My ears burned red with embarrassment and I gritted my teeth.

Luckily, Archie hadn't quite heard what Leonardo said.

But Pu had.

And he was grinning at me like a panting hyena.

I looked down at my hands and kept eating.

"I heard somewhere that whoever yields properly to fate is deemed wise among men, and knows the laws of heaven," Leonardo continued, smiling at me.

"Ugh. That again," Archie groaned. "Not you, too."

"How about you tell us what task you want us to accomplish, Leo? Or are you just going to feed us until we're fat enough to be served as a hearty Thanksgiving feast?" Pu asked. "If we leave Archie alone with these pastries any longer, we're going to have to look up if gods can get diabetes."

"Well, when you put it that way, how can I ignore such an eloquent plea?" Leonardo asked. "Let's see, a task. A task. Well, I do enjoy having my own prison where practically no one visits me. Except for you poor souls and a few select friends, of course. My only problem with this place is the dust. I can't keep it clean, and I have just the most-wretched allergies. Even when I *try* to clean, I just stir up all the dust and I am left coughing and hacking with red burning eyes for a week."

"Am I supposed to feel sorry for you, Old Man?" Pu asked. "Dust? Boo-whooo-whoo."

"Well, my dust story brings us to your task, you ingrate. I want you guys to clean this whole place and make it *stay* clean," Leonardo said.

"Clean your house? Forever? For-ever-ever?" I asked, very confused, as we couldn't really be live-in maids for eternity.

We couldn't, right?

"Oh, and the prisons. The dust there keeps coming over here, too. The whole place needs a good cleaning," Leonardo answered.

I looked at Archie and Pu with wide eyes.

"And then I'll give you the work of art you need in order to leave this place and go back to the game board," Leonardo said, setting another plate of finger sandwiches on the table, and moving the plate of pastries away from Archie.

"I see," Archie replied, moving the plate of pastries back toward himself.

"What do you see?" I asked. "I see insanity. We can't clean this whole prison and keep it clean forever. That's supernatural. Humans can't do that."

"Well, strictly speaking, there aren't any humans here," Pu said.

"We need a vacuum," Archie said. "A huge vacuum that just runs on its own."

"But then how does it clean itself?" Leonardo asked. "If it runs on its own, then the bag will get full and then it will stop working."

He tapped his chin, thinking hard.

Men are nuts.

I mean—sorry—*these* men are nuts.

Not all men.

Cough.

"I have a question," I interrupted this ridiculous conversation. "If we're inside a series of prints created by this other lejerdemani artist dude, what is this made out of? This black and white world? How could it possibly have dust?

Isn't it imaginary?"

"No, it's not imaginary," Leonardo replied. "It all exists. It just exists in a different way than your Earthly home Realm exists."

"So what is this world made out of that it produces dust?" I asked.

"Well, ink, my dear," Leonardo said.

"Ink?" I asked.

"Yes, ink. Made from soot, turpentine, walnut oil, usually," Leonardo explained.

"So the dust is really ink dust, right?" I asked.

Archie, Pu, and Leonardo all looked at me, seemingly surprised that I had come to that conclusion.

"Yes, yes I guess it is," Leonardo answered.

"So there's all this ink dust accumulating. Does that mean this world is falling apart? Crumbling? And it won't exist after a while?" I asked.

"No. It will exist forever here, because it's part of the Realm of Destruction. Everything exists forever here," Archie said, shaking his head. "The dust is just normal dust. But it happens to be in a print. So it's ink dust."

"Alright. So what if we get an army of high-powered robotic vacuums that just buzz around everywhere, sucking up the ink dust. And then they poop it back out as ink pens. That way the vacuums don't have bins that get full," I said.

Archie, Pu, and Leonardo looked at me again, seemingly surprised that I had come up with that idea.

"Someone has created a game where her special brand of stupid is actually useful. I'm not sure who to pity more right now," Pu said.

"Special brand of stupid? *Yeesh*, no. That's very smart, my dear!" Leonardo said. "I haven't seen a robotic vacuum with my own eyes. But they sound fantastic and I was planning on getting one. And I always have to order more pens, so this will be wonderful!"

"If we can get it to work," Pu mumbled.

"I can get it to work," Archie replied.

"Oh yes, the boy genius who let his powers be stolen by Mr. Tizzy-Pants-Lontano," Pu said and sighed. "*You'll* be able to get it to work?"

"Well, we just have to get the vacuums though," Archie replied, unfazed by the insults. "I can't cast a spell to create hundreds of vacuums. Not without possibly calling up Lontano. In my current state...."

"And what state is that again, exactly?" Pu interjected. "The state of uselessness?"

"You're being a royal pill," I said as I poked Pu in the side.

"That's kinda my *raison d'etre*," he replied. "And where does boy genius expect to get hundreds of vacuums if he can't cast a spell to create them?"

"A factory warehouse?" I asked, joking.

"Ooooooo," Pu replied. "Can we get to one of those? I mean, you can't buy them at a warehouse. But maybe we can, like, leave something behind in their place as a payment?"

"Ah, I can give you something to leave behind," Leonardo said.

He walked over to a cupboard and took out a notebook.

"I've been putting doodles in this one for the past month. But according to my friends, even my inane doodles fetch quite a bit of money on the market nowadays," Leonardo said. "So leave this one behind in exchange for the vacuums."

"One of Leonardo's drawings would probably sell for over $3 million right now," Pu said. "So I think we can just take one sheet from that notebook."

My mouth went dry. 3 million? Dollars? Did he actually mean dollars? Or, like, yen?

"Wait," I said as I realized that they had not

taken my factory warehouse joke as a joke.

"What?" Pu asked.

"So a cat with pink underwear on its head, a weird absurdly attractive guy in a tux, the ghost of Leonardo da Vinci, and an odd girl are going to break into a warehouse—even though we're stuck in this game—and walk out with 900 vacuums? While also leaving behind a Leonardo da Vinci sketch worth $3 million? And then we just expect that the person who finds the drawing will know what it is and what it's worth?" I asked in the most incredulous tone I could muster.

"Yeah, sounds good to me," Pu said, nodding.

"*Aaaand* you don't see any flaws to this plan?" I prompted.

"I could leave a handwritten note saying that it's a genuine Leonardo da Vinci sketch," Leonardo added.

"Which I think will then lead them to the conclusion that it is, in fact, *not* a Leonardo sketch and it's all just been a horrible crime-slash-prank," I replied. "Let's go back to step one, though. How do we get out of the game and go to a warehouse?"

Pu looked at Archie.

I looked at Archie.

Leonardo looked at Archie.

"Ah, yes," Archie said, nodding. "I see your point now. We can't leave the game without possibly pulling Lontano to us. Right. Hmmm."

"It's a good thing you're dishy," Pu mumbled. "Or else you'd be entirely pointless."

"Alright, alright. Let's think about this rationally. If that's possible," I said as I stared into my tea, trying to assemble the pieces of the puzzle in my mind. "If I could cast a Force of Virtue icon that brought out an actual flesh-and-blood person-thing, who then called up the game board pieces, is there an equivalent for stealing something? I mean, Belly-fun probably isn't going to see stealing vacuums as virtuous, so he's not gonna show up for that kind of party, right? But maybe we can call up someone who would have the ability to leave the game and steal the vacuums safely, because he or she isn't bonded to Lontano."

"Okay, okay. That's it. Leo, did you somehow slip liquid intelligence into her tea?" Pu asked. "Stella, when did you become smart? I've sat in your head for over a decade and this is the first time you've had two good thoughts back to back."

I sighed.

"An icon? Well, there's Furto," Leonardo said. "He's the Icon of Theft. Stella could call upon him to steal the vacuums."

And for a brief moment, I wondered why we hadn't started this "obtaining" vacuums conversation with a discussion of Furto. I also thought about the possibility of using Furto to steal answer keys for my upcoming math tests.

I mean, no. I didn't think that.

That would be immoral. Cough.

"Do you guys think he'll be able to get hundreds of vacuums without an issue?" I asked.

"Well, that I don't know. I've never actually asked an icon to do anything," Leonardo said, shaking his head.

"I'm sure Furto can steal anything, as long as you have the space for the stolen items," Archie replied.

"Alright, so let's dial him up and get this show on the road," I said, sounding more confident than I felt.

"No, no. You can only fully-cast one icon per day," Pu said, shaking his head.

"Really? Is that true?" I asked. "I thought you

didn't know about this casting icon stuff, Pu."

"No. It's not true. But I'm tired and I want to go to sleep. You people might not realize it but it's way *way* past my bedtime. Do you really think I can just go-go-go for 24 hours straight or something?" Pu grumbled. "That's the problem with these 'life-or-death' plots—no one sleeps or poops or pees. And they rarely ever eat. Like that stuff just doesn't happen. But it has to. I mean, if we're living, breathing beings we need to poop, pee, sleep, and eat. Maybe the author thinks that it's unimportant to the plot or something and everyone just *assumes* that's all happening even though they aren't reading about it. But I still need to sleep, even if Maple doesn't want to write about me sleeping."

We all looked at Pu.

And we waited for Maple to say something.

(Maple: But I didn't say anything because I didn't want to acknowledge Pu's insolence.

Pu: But you just said something.

Maple: *Dammit*. Gosh, fine. You can all go to sleep now. Yeesh.)

"I have a guest suite," Leonardo offered, winking at Archie. "For these types of occasions when the characters need to rest because it's past their bedtime."

I couldn't tell if he was being patronizing or just fulfilling a need in the plot, but we finished up our high tea and then he led us to the guest suite.

Which contained a red velvet bed in the shape of a heart.

(Stella: Is this your idea of a joke, Maple?

Maple: Of course. But I could've made it much worse. Like rose petals on the comforter. And....

Stella: Stop.)

"This is wonderful!" Pu proclaimed. "Is there an outside lock on the door?"

"Yep," Leonardo said.

"Great!" Pu said.

Then he pulled Leonardo out of the room by his bootlace, closed the door, and the lock clicked into place.

Wait, what just happened?

"Very funny guys!" Archie called out as he banged his fist against the door and tried to open it. "Unlock the door!"

"Nooooppppppeeee!!!!" Leonardo and Pu sang in unison.

"This is insane!" Archie almost screamed. "*What even is this room?* This is perverted!"

"It's Raphael's room when he stays here. And yes, it is perverted," Leonardo said. "Have a very lovely night! Pu and I will return for you in the morning."

"Maybe a few mornings from now," Pu added.

I broke into a cold sweat, and started looking for a place to hide. Was there enough space underneath the bed for me to fit?

Archie continued knocking and pulling on the door. But it wasn't opening. Then he tried to cast a spell to unlock it. Judging by his subsequent swearing, it didn't work.

"I'll just blow it up," he said, readying himself to cast a more powerful spell.

"If you do that, won't Lontano know where you are?" I asked.

"Maybe," he said, as he paused. "Good point."

"Should *I* try to unlock it with a spell?" I asked.

"No, no. That might take a while. You should rest," he said.

He was probably scared I would blow up both of us along with the door.

Then he stared at the floor, while I tried to stare at the ceiling. But my gaze kept creeping back to him.

"I'll sleep on the couch," he said as he grabbed a blanket from the foot of the bed, and planted himself on the sofa.

Which was really a heart-shaped loveseat.

I tried not to think too much about what this room's purpose was, but it was kind of obvious.

"Uhhhh, this bed is almost as big as this room. I think it's two king-size beds put together. It's big enough to share. Big enough for two of us," I said, feeling bad that he was going to scrunch up for the night on a loveseat.

"No, no," Archie said, shaking his head. "I'll sleep here. It's fine."

"Ahh. Okay," I said after some nervous laughter.

*Oh. Thank. God.*

I had automatically said the polite thing without thinking of the possible consequences.

*How stupid could I be?*

Sleep on the same bed with him for the night?

How would that work? I'd had an irregular heartbeat because of him ever since we landed in this game, and I was supposed to somehow survive lying next to him in the same bed? Clearly I was insane. There's no ER in this game, Stella. You can't have a cardiac event in here.

I walked over to the nightstand lamp to turn it off, but then thought better of that. Let's not sleep in the dark in this situation. Then I scrambled into the massive bed of love, and hid under the red velvet blankets of love.

Several moments passed as I listened to my furiously beating heart and slowly ran out of fresh air underneath the blankets. Eventually I had to poke my head out or risk self-suffocation.

As I took in a few lung-fulls of fresh air, I made eye contact with Archie. He had been watching me from the loveseat. But he quickly looked away.

That's it.

*I'm going to go insane.*

He'd totally been looking at me. Even though I was just a lump in the bed, he'd been looking at me. God, does my butt look gigantic like this? Is there a way to make my hips look smaller if I change the way I'm laying down? How can I possibly fall asleep? What if I snore while I'm out? Or drool? Or fart?

That's it.

*I'm going to go insane.*

# CHAPTER SEVEN.

*Various Late Night Thoughts.*

<u>Archie's Late Night Thoughts</u>

I wonder. I wonder if the spell is gone for good? If I touch her again will she start acting weird? Or is it gone? I find it hard to believe that an itzal izaki's spell would only last for such a short amount of time. But then again, she is the Jainko-hiltzaile. So perhaps her powers cancelled out Pu's powers?

And is the spell truly triggered by all men or just me?

And will she fall in love with all men?

Or just me?

*Wait, what's wrong with me?*

Never mind. Never mind.

But what if I just touched her hair?

Would that count as touching? Would that trigger it?

*Wait, again—what's wrong with me?*

Delete that last part about the hair-touching.

Ugh, it's too late. It's already in the story. *Dammit.*

Stella's Late Night Thoughts

I'm going to have a freaking cardiac event even without an ER.

He keeps smacking his lips.

Or clicking his tongue.

Or doing something with his mouth that's making a noise and it's driving me nuts.

Oh, god. He just sighed.

Why is *he* sighing?

I'm the one dying over here.

I'm so freaking hot right now. I can't stay under these blankets. I have to kick them off. But then he'll be able to see my huge butt.

Okay, I'll lay flat on the bed. Then he can't see my butt even if I kick off the blankets.

Archie's Late Night Thoughts

Why'd she kick off the blankets?

Is she mad at me because I was looking at her?

Is she feeling okay?

Is she too hot?

I wonder if she has a fever?

Why is she laying so stiffly like there's a wooden board underneath her?

Doesn't that hurt her back lying like that?

Stella's Late Night Thoughts

Oh, god! My back hurts!

I can't keep lying like this or I'll die from the pain.

"Stuffing marshmallow salts!" I said as I sat up like a shot. "*Why'd you tell me not to touch any men, not even you?!*"

Yes, that had been bugging me.

I admit that.

"Ummmm," was his highly intelligent reply.

"No, no. Don't answer that," I said. "Never mind. Don't tell me."

"Ummmm."

How was I possibly going to fall asleep now? Someone was going to have to chloroform me for me to even be able to close my eyes.

Breathe, Stella. Breathe and calm down.

"Can I touch your hair?" he asked. "No. Never mind. Don't let me touch your hair. That's a bad idea. Ignore that."

*What the?*

I had stopped breathing.

My brain was about to explode.

Ignore that?

How could I possibly ignore that?

Touch my hair?

Was that perverted?

No—right?

It's normal for people to touch each other's hair, right?

Right?

"Is there something wrong with my hair?" I asked.

"No, no. Not at all. It's not that."

That's not it?

Then what the heck is it????

*Then. What. The. Heck. Is. It????*


Archie's Late Night Thoughts

*What the heck was that?!?*

Touch her hair???

Was I insane?

That sounded so perverted.

And what good would touching her hair do?

I certainly shouldn't be testing the spell in a

locked room.

I need to keep my mouth shut.


<u>Stella's Late Night Thoughts</u>

Why does he want to touch my hair?

Why?

Why? Why? Why? *Whyyyyyyyyyyy?*

Okay, think about something else Stella. Think about something else or you're going to have an aneurysm.

What else is there to think about?

Archie.

Yeah, I'll think about Archie.

Wait, that'll just bring me back to the hair thing.

Something else. Something else.

Why, why, why....

"Why do you wear a tuxedo? Isn't that kind of a random outfit to wear?"

Wait, where did that come from???

"Ummmm. It's my armor. Sort of."

"Armor?"

"I—uh—find that most people don't approach me when I'm in a tuxedo. It keeps them at arm's length."

"Why keep people at arm's length? You don't

like people?"

"Most people? No. I don't like them. Some people? Yes. But I know very few people."

"On purpose?"

"On purpose."

He was certainly an odd duck, this guy. He hadn't given off the vibe that he didn't like people. Or had he? If so, I guess I had missed those signals.

"Am I one of those people you don't like? Or one of those people you do like?" I asked.

Why did I do that?

Why did I ask that?

Oh my god. It was my blabbermouth disease striking again. I couldn't keep my mouth shut when I really, *really* needed to keep my mouth shut. Stop being nervous. Stop being nervous! How in the world was that going to be possible given this situation?!?!

"Wait, don't tell me. That was a bad idea. Ignore that," I said. "I'm gonna turn off the lights and neither one of us can say anything more once it's dark. Okay? Okay."

I flipped off the nightstand lamp. The room sank into darkness. But I could still sense Archie's presence, lying on the loveseat. Breathing.

Blinking. Existing. Ten or so feet away from me. I laid back down in bed and listened to my hormonal heart steadily thump itself toward exhaustion.

I really, *really* want to fast-forward through these awkward teen years to the point where I'm an adult who has her life together and I can actually manage to be in the same room with a male, alone, without losing my mind.

Is that possible? No? Yes? Maybe?

Ugh, why am I even here?

Why? Why? *Why?*

"So if my mother didn't give birth to me, but yet I'm here and I'm her daughter—how did that happen?"

"Um. Isn't the light off? Are we *not* talking in the dark? Or are we talking? Should I answer that question?"

"Do you know the answer?"

"No."

"No, I guess you wouldn't, would you. It's not like you were around for that."

"I was around, but not present for that. I didn't know your mother, and I just met your father for the first time."

He was around?

He was alive?

How old was he at the time?

Stop wondering about that Stella.

Yeesh, let's just accept the fact that he's way older than me and move on with our life. Old or young or whatever, this guy is just way, *way, waaaaayyyy* too attractive to ever be with me. There's feasible. And there's unfeasible. And him being with me would definitely land in the unfeasible category. No feas present, at all, ever. *Ever ever.*

# CHAPTER EIGHT.

*At the Mysterious Well with the Mysterious Nutjob.*

*By Morrow.*

"So we're playing the Game of Goose right now?" I asked our teddy bear informant.

"Yes, you are. Duh," the lobster chimed in. "And you must've landed on The Well. So that's why you're at a—*well.* Get it???"

"Ugh, I don't have time for this," Lontano said, still crying. "I have to find Archie and kill him."

"I know I'm the one who did this to you, but I can't stand your crying anymore. Don't say I never did anything for you," Nora said to Lontano, as she took pity on him and removed the 'cry over spilled milk' spell.

He just glared at her as he wiped his nose on his

bathrobe sleeve.

"Do you know where Archie is?" I asked The Well's inhabitants.

"He's at The Prison," the teddy bear answered. "Which one? I have no clue. There are thousands of them connected to the game."

"Well, at least, how do we get out of here and go back to the game board place where George was?" Nora asked.

"You have to play the game to go back. You must complete the task set for you by the lejerdemani ghost who lives here and then you'll be allowed to go back," the lobster said.

"I hate this stupid game," Lontano said and sighed, as he sat down on the ground.

"So where's the lejerdemani ghost?" I asked, noting that Ellie had turned pale at the word 'ghost.'

"Well, Mother Shipton's ghost lives in the little black and white cottage at the front of the park. She's not a lejerdemani ghost, but she'd know where you could find one," the teddy bear said. "Asking her is probably faster than roaming around the whole wood looking for one."

"Why is my life always so tiresome?" Lontano asked—no one in particular, I guess.

"Is that a metaphorical question?" I asked.

"You mean rhetorical question, Morrow," Ellie said, making me feel dumb.

"It's probably both," he answered as he laid down on the ground and curled up into a ball.

"Is he okay?" the lobster asked. "He seems a bit weird."

"That's because he *is* a bit weird," Nora said.

"Well, do we go to the cottage to find Mother Shipton and just leave him here or bring him with us?" I asked.

"I think it's better to take him with us so we can keep an eye on him," Ellie answered. "I'd like to *know* what he's doing rather than *guess* what he's doing, given the fact that he's a nutjob."

"You just want to keep him around so you can keep drooling over him," I whispered.

"Is there something wrong with that?" she whispered back.

"Well, it's true," Nora said. "If we don't keep him with us, we have no idea what kind of stuff he's getting up to. And if he manages to track down Archie, Stella, and Pu because he's bonded to Archie—well, I don't want to be wandering around looking for ghosts while that happens."

"I'm not going anywhere," Lontano interjected. "I'm going to lie here until I get zapped somewhere else. Eventually I'll meet up with that turdhole again, and then he and I can finally settle this like men."

"For someone with a tear-stained face lying in his bathrobe in the fetal position in the dirt, I'm not sure the words 'finally settle this like men' should be coming out of your mouth," Nora said.

"Why are you antagonizing him?" I asked. "I don't think that's exactly a wise approach."

"Fine. C'mon. I won't harass you, Lontano. Just follow us to the cottage," Nora said.

"No," he replied.

"Follow in my footsteps, my handsome man," Ellie purred another idiom spell onto Lontano, although I'm not sure he even noticed that it happened.

She started walking in the direction the teddy bear and lobster had told us to go, and Lontano automatically got up off the ground and followed her every footstep. Whether he wanted to or not.

"Start walking funny and jumping around so he has to follow those movements," Nora suggested.

"I'm not interested in looking like an idiot,"

Ellie replied.

"Man, I am. I wish I had cast the spell, instead," Nora said and sighed. "I would've had him dancing a jig by now."

"Again, why are you antagonizing him?" I asked.

"I'm going to pretend that I'm following you of my own volition," Lontano said. "Are you three ever going to tell me who you are?"

"No," Nora answered.

"Goddesses of Mischief?" he asked.

"Well…" Nora said. "You can call us that if you want. It works fine for me."

"I'll be your Goddess of Love," Ellie suggested.

"Stop that," I interrupted her. "I think a more important topic to discuss right now would be: what did you do to Penny, Eagle, and Derek?"

"What did I do to them? Hmmmmm," Lontano said, and smiled. "Who are they?"

"Two lejerdemani and the rabbit that you—did something to," I said.

"How would I know about them?" he asked.

"Do you really want me to cast a spell where you have to answer every question I ask you truthfully. Because I can do that. And it's never very pretty," I said.

"Fine, fine. Fine, fine. Fine," he replied. "I transformed them into porcelain figurines, and with your skills—well, you may be able to transform them back. If you ever find them that is. They're somewhere in the House of Coventry. But that place will never give up its secrets to you. So if you want to see them again, I suggest you play nicely with me."

"That's what I've been thinking about doing all along," Ellie said and smiled, non-innocently.

"You're not allowed to talk anymore," I told her. "Lontano, if you give us back Penny, Eagle, and Derek in their normal forms, like they were before, what do you want in return?"

"Already beginning to negotiate with me? That's a bit daring, don't you think? What use could you three possibly have with such useless lejerdemani?"

"Like I said, what do you want in return? You must want something. If you don't, why'd you kidnap Stella?"

"You didn't kidnap her because you wanted her for yourself, right?" Ellie interrupted. "It's not like you're in love with her, are you? She's not that attractive. And she's supposed to end up with Archie."

"Would you shut up?" I said to her.

"In love with Stella?" Lontano asked. "Am I? Well, that sounds absurd. Absurdly delicious! And if Archie wants her, then I definitely have to make her mine. But then again, I don't know. What do I know? Oh yes, I know that I wanted Stella to save my sister, who is inside of me right now."

"YOU ATE YOUR SISTER?!" Nora asked.

"No. Not really."

Ellie stopped walking, turned around, and stared at Lontano.

I blinked at him, rapidly.

And Nora scratched her head.

"*Not really?*" she asked.

"Well, *not really*. Anyway, given your abilities, maybe the *three of you* can fix my sister," he added and smiled excitedly. "Yes, yes. If you do that, I'll give you those lejerdemani and that rabbit."

"Your sister is inside of you right now?" Ellie asked. "Did I hear that correctly?"

"Are you sure you didn't eat her?" Nora asked, in a disgusted—but simultaneously fascinated—tone of voice.

"Yes, no. I mean, no I didn't eat her. Her soul

is inside of me in a little glass vial, along with seven other demi-god souls. I ate those vials. They power my skeleton spell. Which I could probably use to defeat you three right now, but for some reason I haven't been able to use it since Archie transformed me back into my flesh and blood version, as he punched me in the face. But don't worry, it could come back at any moment and then I'll rip you apart from limb to limb and this conversation will no longer seem important."

Um.

"How comforting," Ellie said. "So, uh, you want to bring her back to life from her vial format?"

"Yes. Exactly."

"Sounds difficult," I said.

"But maybe not impossible," Nora said. "If you don't kill us, then we'll see what we can do about fixing your sister. But we'd need Penny, Eagle, and Derek for that kind of thing."

"Oh, you three are so tiresome. Asking for your half of the deal to be served to you even before you deliver on your part? What kind of idiocy is that?"

"Well, we still need to get out of this game in

order to do anything," I said. "Then we can argue about who owes who what and when, when we're actually back at the House of Coventry."

After some more grumbling and bickering, we arrived at the black-and-white checkered cottage and knocked on the door. The portrait of Mother Shipton on the bulletin board by the park entrance showed her as a nasty old hag, with stringy grey hair, a big nose, and the wrinkled, warty face typical of a witch.

The Mother Shipton that answered the door was a heavily mascaraed teenage girl in a denim mini skirt and light grey t-shirt, with a high-ponytail and big gold hoop earrings. She held a giant bowl of bright yellow popcorn. In between shoving handfuls of popcorn into her mouth, she asked us: "What?"

"Um, Mother Shipton?" I asked.

"Yeah, that's me. Whatcha want?"

I forgot what I wanted. I was so confused.

"Where's the lejerdemani ghost in this god-forsaken park?" Lontano asked.

Mother Shipton stopped chewing, and looked him up and down.

"Are you some kind of pervert?" she asked.

"Yes," Nora answered firmly.

"Noooo," Ellie replied.

"Why's he in a bathrobe and nothing else?" Mother Shipton asked.

"Because, I'm a pervert. Can we come inside your house?" Lontano asked.

"Sure, I guess," Mother Shipton replied.

We all shuffled into the cottage, and awkwardly arranged ourselves on the living room furniture. Ellie considered sitting next to Lontano on the largest sofa, but then thought better of it and joined Nora on the loveseat. So Lontano draped himself over the whole sofa, barely managing to keep his robe closed. Although he didn't seem to care about that one way or the other. I claimed the overstuffed chair, and Mother Shipton situated herself in her desk chair, by her computer, which appeared to have a MMORPG up on the screen. She continued hoovering up the popcorn while she gave Lontano the stink-eye.

"I apologize for our pushy intrusion," he said. "But I hate standing."

"I have a question for you. Why don't you look like the Mother Shipton on the sign outside?" Nora asked. "You don't look old, or even like you're from the old timey times."

"Ghosts can look however they want to look," she replied. "I'm certainly not going to look like that poster for the rest of eternity. Can you imagine going down in history as being famously hideous? Do you know what that does to a woman's ego?"

"You look fine to me," Lontano said.

"Keep your skeevy eyeballs to yourself, mister," she replied.

"I can't win. Anyway. Lejerdemani ghost. Where is it? Hmmmm?" he asked.

"So you guys must be playing the Game of Goose?"

"Yes, yes. So we need that stupid ghost for the stupid game," Lontano said, snapping his fingers, repeatedly, being extra-annoyingly arrogant.

"Hmmm, well, yeah. There is one of those here," Mother Shipton said. "Or else the game wouldn't have sent you here in the first place. But I kinda know what he'd ask you to help him with, and I don't want you guys to help him with that. So I kinda don't want to tell you where he is."

"Why do I feel like this conversation just ended?" Nora asked.

"Wait, why don't you want us to help him?" I

asked.

"Because he'd ask you to defeat my team in this game we play. He always loses to me and my guys. But why would I want to lose? I wouldn't—ya see? Besides, I only started playing this thing because I wanted to troll him. He moved into my park, and didn't even ask if he could live here. Never said a word to me. So I decided to kick his butt in the game he's obsessed with. He doesn't even know it's me. If you help him, all my fun is over."

"This is absurd," Lontano said.

"Life is nothing, if not absurd," Mother Shipton replied.

"That game on your screen?" Ellie asked. "That's the game you play?"

"Yeah, you know it?" Mother Shipton asked.

My sisters and I exchanged knowing looks with each other. The look of knowing that Penny had limited our daily screen time to the point where we were not MMORPG experts. At all. Our skill level was at the grade where we knew what a MMORPG was.

"Are you really sure he'll ask for our help winning this game against you? He might want something else," Ellie suggested.

"No. I know what he wants. He wants to win," Mother Shipton said.

"Well, there must be something you want more than just to troll him, right? What can we do for you in exchange for you possibly losing?" I asked, knowing full well that if we managed to win this game against this girl that the heavens would open up and angels would start singing hymns in our name because it would be a freckin' miracle.

"Hmmm. He's got to teach me how to draw," Mother Shipton said. "He's right there. He's super-famous. And yet he refuses to even talk with me. I wanted drawing lessons in exchange for him squatting on my property. But he told me to leave him alone. So if he wins, he's got to teach me how to draw."

"How do we say we'll help him if he teaches you how to draw?" Ellie asked. "When we're supposed to be just doing a task for him to move forward in the game?"

"Eh, we'll cross that bridge when we get to it," Nora interjected. "For now we can make the deal that if we beat you in this game for him, he'll teach you how to draw, right?"

"Yeah. Deal," Mother Shipton said and nodded.

"This is absurd," Lontano repeated.

Mother Shipton then explained that the ghost in question lived in the park's cave, which was exactly in the direction we had come from. Wonderful. She also explained that it would soon be nighttime, and walking around out there in the dark probably would lead to us drowning in the river. Wonderful. So she further explained that we should go across the street and stay for the night at the inn because she didn't have enough room in her cottage for four more people to sleep there, especially if one of them was a pervert. Wonderful.

Feeling ever-so-slightly like we'd just been kicked out of Mother Shipton's house, we made our way across the street to the inn-pub thingy, where everyone shared a look of bewilderment at the man in his bathrobe accompanied by three children. But luckily they still had one room left to give us for the night, and dinner was being served.

The owner sat us in the back room, away from most of the customers. Probably on purpose. Only two men were back there, both of whom seemed ecstatic to see Lontano. 'Seemed' being the key word. It was definitely excitement designed to mask wariness.

"Oh, ho, ho! My dear maggoty sir! What has happened to you???" the one with the fierce long nose asked Lontano, marveling at his dirtied bathrobe and disheveled appearance.

"Nothing, Perdita, nothing. Don't ask. I have suffered too much to even relate the tale," Lontano said as he sat down at their table.

"Who are these lovely lasses?" the second man asked.

"Nothing, Puggy, nothing. Don't ask. I have suffered too much to even relate the tale," Lontano repeated, sighing. "Trust me, you don't want anything to do with them."

The three men had dinner together, while us three misfits ate at another table, and eavesdropped on their conversation. Well, the bits and pieces we could hear, at least. I thought about casting an enhanced hearing spell, but decided I shouldn't risk ticking off Lontano. I preferred him when he wasn't an angry sofa-punching maniac.

We shyly inquired with our server about who the two men were and learned that they were the ghosts of Thomas Gainsborough, aka Perdita, and J.M.W. Turner, aka Puggy.

"Both artists," Ellie said. "Possibly lejerde-mani? I'm not sure how we can tell that though since Lontano's aura is too strong and it's pretty much all I can get a reading on. But they would know how to draw."

"Possibly useful," Nora whispered. "How do we trick them into helping us?"

"These moldwarps will go with us tomorrow to the cave. Apparently Michelangelo is squatting there and they're planning on visiting him. Mikey is the ghost we have to see to complete the task," Lontano said as he leaned back in his chair toward our table.

"That was easy," Nora said.

"Has he been listening to us the whole time he's been talking with them?" I whispered.

"Yes," Lontano answered.

My sisters and I finished our meal in silence.

Perdita and Puggy stayed downstairs after dinner, while the four of us retreated to our room, which luckily had two beds in it.

"You could stay with those two guys," I suggested to Lontano, as I examined how close the two beds actually were.

"I'd rather you three weren't alone," he replied. "Especially with those two moldwarps here. You three Goddesses of Mischief can handle yourselves, but I still need to safeguard my territory. Plus, that following the leader spell or whatever the heck you cast is still in effect, so I can't go anywhere that the tall one doesn't go."

He pointed to Ellie. Who was apparently the tall one.

"She's only half an inch taller than me," Nora said, obviously flustered.

"Yes. Like that matters. Wake me up in 9 hours, no more, no less," Lontano said, dismissing her whining, as he took off his slippers, and got into bed.

He wrapped himself into a blanket cocoon up over his head until only his bare feet were showing.

"But!" he announced from under the blankets. "Don't think I've just accepted this situation! I'm still trying to figure out who or what you three things are and how to destroy you. And I'll figure everything out. Eventually."

My sisters and I looked at each other, but stayed quiet. There were three choices in this scenario. 1) Say something that will antagonize him. Too risky. 2) Say something that will appease him. Too nauseating. 3) Say nothing. Best to go with that one.

Within a few minutes he started snoring, and we watched him for a while in silence. It was like a raccoon had entered our house and was peacefully snoozing in the corner. He seemed to pose no immediate threat to us—as he was asleep. And yet you couldn't really take your eyes off of him. And you couldn't really go to sleep yourself for fear of what he might do while you were off in slumberland.

"We'll each take one three-hour shift watching him," Ellie said, as Nora and I nodded in agreement. "I'll go first."

"No touching him, Ellie," I added.

She pouted in response.

# CHAPTER NINE.

*Furto, The Icon of Theft.*

*By Stella Asswiper Grum.*

(Maple: Asswiper is from Old English. It means 'Donkey Resistance,' jfyi. So Stella's people probably led a donkey rebellion, once upon a time. Also, by now I hope you realize that I am full of doodoo, jfyi.

Stella: I realized that a long time ago. So the readers are probably also aware of that fact. But more importantly, can I get a real middle name?

Maple: How about Donkey-Queen?)

*Furto: Theft.*
*A pale Youth, clothed with a Wolf's*
*Skin, his Arms and Legs bare;*
*wing'd Feet; at midnight; in one Hand a*
*Purse, and a Knife in the other,*

*with a Picklock; the Ears of a Hare,*
*and seems to be in Fear.*
*Youth shows Imprudence, that will not*
*take Warning; the Paleness,*
*and Hares Ears, continual Suspicion and*
*Fear, and therefore loves Darkness;*
*The Skin, because the Wolf lives by Rapine.*
*The Bareness shows him in*
*Distress; and the wing'd Feet, his flying from Justice.*

The next morning, after a mostly sleepless night, Archie and I emerged from the guest bedroom both worse for the wear. Leonardo had unlocked the door and informed us that he had prepared a hearty breakfast, which Pu was already devouring by the time we got to the kitchen.

"How'd it go last night, guys?" Pu asked, and then smiled gleefully. "Did you manage to trigger the spell again Archie?"

"Trigger the spell?" I asked, joining him at the table.

"Sssshhhhhh," Archie replied, as he shoved a hashbrown into Pu's mouth.

"Thanks," Pu responded after he chewed. "Well, what happened?"

"Ssshhh," Archie repeated. "Nothing happened. Let's just eat breakfast."

"Nothing? *Nothing?!* What? *Really?* That's terribly disappointing," Pu said.

I looked at Pu, who was glaring at Archie.

I looked at Archie, who was beginning to eat his weight in scones.

And I looked at Leonardo, who smiled warmly at me in return.

"Do you know what's going on?" I asked him.

"No, he doesn't. Sshhhh," Archie said, glancing at Leonardo, who then shrugged in response. "But. Yeah. When we call on Furto, make sure you don't touch him at all, Stella."

And back to the no-touching directive we went.

"No, no. Touch Furto a lot," Pu instructed. "*Like a ton.* Like definitely."

"No, don't touch him at all. Ever," Archie said.

"But how will we know if the spell works on other men, or just you?" Pu asked.

"We don't need to know that, at all. Ever," Archie answered.

I had been intrigued. But now I was intrigued and a bit panicky. What was this spell? What had happened in the prison cell? What couldn't I remember?

"Stella, this is for your own good," Archie continued. "Don't touch Furto."

We shared a brief moment of eye contact; I wasn't sure if he was angry or about to cry. Then he went back to the scones.

Pu nudged me with his foot, winked at me, and made a kissy face.

After we gorged ourselves on scones, Leonardo plopped a large, leather-bound book on the table. It opened itself and flipped its pages lazily.

"Hurry up," Leonardo told the book. "This isn't the time to be sleepy."

The page flipping sped up and then stopped.

"Furto," Leonardo read aloud. "Well, in summary of the Italian, he's a young man. Pale. He wears a wolf skin as a coat. His feet are winged. His ears are rabbit ears. He usually has a bag, a knife, and a lock pick. He'll only show up if it's dark in the room. And he's generally fidgety, rash, and scared of everything."

"So imagine all of that Stella, while reciting his name out loud, and then we can get this show on the road," Pu said.

Leonardo snapped his fingers, turning off the lights. Archie nervously tapped his fingers on the table. Pu made obscene farty noises with his mouth. I closed my eyes and tried to imagine the young man Leonardo had described. He sounded kinda terrifying, so it was with some hesitation.

A bunny man dressed as a wolf who steals things? Um.

"Oh, and I've read that when he's around everyone near him becomes a klepto. So hold on to your belongings, and keep your eyes peeled," Leonardo said.

"We'll what?" I asked as my bracelet began to heat up again to the point of burning my skin.

A beam of light shot from it and out popped Furto. Or who I assumed was Furto.

"Ugh god, it's too bright in here," he said as he dragged a chair over to the darkest corner of the room and sat down like he owned the place. Then he looked straight at me. "I'd love to sit next to you, sweetheart—you're adorable. But it's not dark enough over there. Feel free to come join me."

Then he winked at me.

Archie cleared his throat.

Furto quickly looked at Archie, Pu, and Leonardo. Then he cracked his neck and took a bag of pastries from his sack. He started eating them like they were potato chips. I really wanted one of those things, or all of them.

Archie was also eyeballing the pastries, while Pu was hiding a napkin and a spoon under his butt, which Leonardo promptly retrieved.

Furto tossed one of the pastries to me, then one to Archie, Pu, and Leonardo.

"I'd rather not be mugged by the God of Destruction and his friends for a Plundergebäck," he said and then continued chewing.

Archie shoved the whole thing in his mouth, started chewing, and then stared at my pastry. So I began to eat mine before he could grab it.

"I guess I should thank you for calling me up, sweetheart," Furto said. "I was stealing these from Mozart and he was about to catch me. Which really wouldn't have been good for my reputation."

"Oh, god! These are delicious," Pu said, as he finished his pastry, the dark fruit filling spilling out onto his tiny furry face.

Then he looked over at Leonardo, who tightened his grip on his own pastry.

Furto then tossed another one to Archie and Pu. He was like a lion-tamer sitting in the corner of the cage, tossing fresh meat to the beasts to make sure that he never became the object of their attention. He lobbed some more pastries to Leonardo and me, which Pu tried to intercept, but Leonardo swatted him away.

I also noticed my own burning desire to steal the pastries from everyone else, even though there was already one in my hand. I guess this is what magically becoming a klepto feels like.

"So what can I do for you guys?" Furto asked, itching his left ear, which was in fact a human-sized rabbit ear, and covering it in crumbs. "Does this beautiful lady have a request for me?"

"Stop calling her adorable, and beautiful, and a lady, and sweetheart," Archie interrupted. "It's getting on my nerves."

"Why, *oh why*, would that be happening?" Pu asked him, grinning. "Is she not those things? Should he call her ugly instead?"

"That's not what I mean and you know it," Archie said.

"Furto and Stella sitting in a tree," Pu began to sing.

"Stop that. It's not appropriate," Archie said.

"Archie and Stella sitting in a tree," Pu sang.

"That's not appropriate either," Archie said.

"Then what *is* appropriate?" Pu asked. "Archie and Furto sitting in a tree…."

Archie interrupted him with a forced cough and a glare.

"Um," I said, as I really, really wanted to shift the direction of this conversation. "Furto, we need you to steal, like, a thousand robotic vacuums. But we'll pay for them by leaving a Leonardo da Vinci sketch behind."

"Well, then that's not really stealing, is it—*sweetheart*?" Furto asked, and clicked his tongue. He definitely shifted his glance to Archie as he said 'sweetheart.' "I mean, that's just buying something in a weird way. I can't do that. I only steal things."

"So we *have* to break the law in order to use you?" I asked.

"Yep, that's kinda how this works."

Both Leonardo and Pu had finished their second pastries and were eyeballing mine, so I tried to eat it as quickly as possible.

"But you can go to the Realm of the Present, steal them, and bring them back here, no problem?" I asked, my mouth full of pastry.

"Yep. Obviously. Are you new at this or something? I guess so. I haven't seen you around before," Furto said as he looked briefly at my rhenium bracelet, my tattooed arms, and then my face. "I'd remember you. The new Jainkohilt-zaile. *Hmm.* We'll probably be seeing a lot of each other from now on."

He grinned at me, but I knew he was really keeping his eye on Archie.

"Why would she see a lot of you?" Archie asked, visibly irritated.

"This *is* interesting," Furto said as he met Archie's glare.

Then he took out his knife to pick Plunder-gebäck pieces from his teeth.

"What's interesting?" Archie asked.

"The fearless God of Destruction seems to be scared of something," Furto answered. "But what is it, exactly?"

Then Furto looked at me and leaned forward in his chair, slightly into the faint light that came in from the window next to us. His gold eyes glinted.

"I'll go get you a thousand vacuums, sweet-heart. But what do I get in return?" he asked, winking at me. Again.

(Stella: Honestly, what's with all the winking in this story? Do a lot of these people have facial tics?

Maple: Maybe.)

"What was that?" Archie asked him. "*What are you doing?*"

Furto then leaned back in his chair and winked at Archie.

"It's called flirting, Suntsitzea," Furto answered. "Look it up in the dictionary."

"Wait, so you want something for helping us?" I asked. "Belly-fun didn't want anything in return. That's not how this works, right?"

"It depends on the icon," Leonardo answered. "Everyone has their own method. Bellerophon is virtuous, sort of, in a way. Furto, well, isn't. So he's probably not going to do something just out of the goodness of his heart. Which there really isn't much goodness there."

"Ouch. Man. That hurts," Furto chuckled, and then looked at me. "So what can *you* give me?"

"She can't give you anything," Archie interjected.

"She can't?" Furto asked. "Then this deal isn't going to get very far."

"I'll give you something instead," Archie said.

"*You?* No. You're too terrifying. You'll just give me a punch to the face. I don't want anything from you. Her on the other hand, well, she seems like she could be even sweeter than those pastries I just ate. I tell you guys what: I'll get the vacuums, if she gives me a kiss."

Furto pointed to me nonchalantly.

"*Yaaassss!!!*" Pu agreed, with marked excitement. "With lots of touching!!"

My brain went silent.

My eyes widened.

I peed myself.

Well, I was pretty sure I peed myself.

At least, if armpits could pee themselves with sweat that was certainly happening. I could feel the perspiration pouring into the fabric of my shirt.

Archie immediately stood up and knocked his chair over.

"Aren't we all beyond this kind of *moronic*, misogynistic device?!" he asked.

"Oh, no, no, no! We aren't!" Furto responded, and he laughed heartily. "But I love your reaction so much, Suntsitzea, that I'll take that as a payment for the vacuums."

He grinned ecstatically at Archie, who seemed both surprised and embarrassed at his own loss of composure. He righted his chair and sat back down without even glancing at me.

Meanwhile, Pu was trying to steal a plate and more silverware off the table by shoving them into my lap to hide them from Leonardo, who was doing his best to stop him.

"Alright kids, I'll be back in a minute," Furto said.

He blew me a kiss as he disappeared in a puff of dark smoke.

Archie quickly stood up and stretched to grab the kiss in the air before it reached me. Gosh, that was adorable.

Wait. Shut up, Stella.

That wasn't adorable at all.

It was hideously unimpressive. That's right. Yes.

Seconds later, Furto was back with a boxed robotic vacuum in his hand, and somewhere on Earth an electronics store warehouse would soon discover a pressing need to order more vacuums.

"The rest are downstairs in the rooms of the prison. Couldn't exactly fit them all up here. How'd I do, my beautiful princess?" he asked, smiling at me, and twitching his ears.

Archie got up, walked over to him, and

reached out for the vacuum. Furto looked at him, but didn't hand it over. So Archie pried it from his hands.

"You did alright. You did fine. Thank you very much," Archie huffed at Furto. "You can go back to what you were doing now."

"Usually I steal something from every place I go," Furto said as he took a step toward me. "But just to show you how much I care I'm not gonna steal anything from you, Miss—what's your name?"

"Her name isn't important," Archie replied, moving between Furto and me.

"Ooohhh, I see," Furto said. "I guess he doesn't think you're important. Well, I do. Perhaps I *will* steal something from you. Maybe your heart?"

Furto swiftly sidestepped Archie and reached to take my hand.

Archie lunged forward to slap his hand away, but as he did, Furto was zapped back into my bracelet.

I swear I could hear him laughing for several seconds after he was gone.

"That son-of-a..." Archie swore under his breath.

My profuse pit-sweating had begun again. Oh

joy.

"I feel like I would've enjoyed all of that a lot more if I hadn't been distracted by my need to harvest utensils from the table," Pu said and sighed.

"It was definitely enjoyable," Leonardo said. "I've never seen Archie so flustered in my life. And Stella, that Furto is attractive in his own way. Were you swayed, my dear?"

Leonardo was smiling at me, but he was really watching Archie's face turn into an even more disgruntled grimace.

"Was I what?" I asked.

"She doesn't know what that means," Pu said, shaking his head. "Leo means—did he actually manage to steal your heart?"

"She wasn't *swayed* by anything, right Stella? Your heart wasn't stolen, right?" Archie asked me, but then his face said, 'Wait, I regret asking these insane questions.'

"I..." I began.

"Nevermind. Alright," Archie interrupted. "Let me just cast a quick spell on these vacuums to get them to be perpetually enchanted and constantly releasing ink pens. Then we can continue forward."

He mumbled to himself as he removed the vacuum from its box, sat down at the table, and examined the manual.

"That whole exchange was perfect for testing my spell. Too bad it wasn't successful," Pu said. "I'm going to have to be more proactive about this."

By dinnertime, Pu, Leonardo, and I had unboxed all of the vacuums—with a little help from magic. And Archie had gotten all of the vacuums up and running, collecting ink dust, and pooping out pens—with even more help from magic. None of which was provided by me, of course. Because I am clueless.

But still. It was my special-kind-of-stupid idea that had solved the issue. I felt satisfied in a way I had never felt satisfied before. And for a split second, or really a nanosecond, I felt a tiny surge of confidence. But it was gone quickly. And within moments it was as if it had never appeared.

In gratitude for a task well accomplished, Leonardo gifted me a shield from the dark wooden cupboard in the corner of the room.

"The Medusa buckler," Archie said, pursed his lips and looked away.

"It returned to my possession several years

ago, I'm afraid," Leonardo said to Archie. "I assume you know why."

"Unfortunately, I don't," Archie said. "Though we can all guess why. I haven't seen or heard from Ozzie for a long time. Riot would know what happened to him, I'm sure. But she's also MIA. Though that's kind of a good thing."

"Sylvie wouldn't have..." Leonardo's voice trailed off.

"No, she wouldn't have," Archie replied. "Never."

"Anybody else feel like they're missing out on a part of this conversation?" Pu stage whispered to me.

"You don't need to know everything, Pu," Archie replied, but he was looking at me as he said it.

I get it. I get it. Keep the teenager in the dark. Typical. But it's not like I couldn't deduce that Ozzie had once owned that shield, and that he didn't anymore, and he's probably dead or something like dead. Of course, I hadn't really followed who Ozzie was in the first place. So it's not like I could really put all of the pieces together. But I wasn't completely dumb.

"Double-tap for a pocket-size version," Leonardo explained as he tapped the shield twice and it shrunk down to fit in his palm. Then he reached to hand the tiniest, cutest shield in the world to me, but Archie took it from him instead, and put it in his inside jacket pocket.

"Just to avoid you touching him," Archie said to me.

"Feel free to come by anytime you want," Leonardo bid us goodbye.

It was kind of an odd thing to say to people leaving a prison.

He had also packaged up some scones and tarts for us, which is also something you don't typically receive when being un-incarcerated.

Back at the game board, George was waiting for our return.

"I've got bad news and bad news. Which do you want first?" George asked.

"Uhhhh," was all I managed.

"The bad news, then," Archie said.

"Tiziano-Lontano-what's-his-face showed up, and is now inside the game as well," George said.

Archie groaned and rolled his eyes, and I got a nervous feeling in my gut.

"And the other bad news?" Pu asked.

"Well, he's with these three girls. But none of

them rolled any dice. So I don't have a clue where they are or what they're doing," George explained. "They were here for an instant, and then they were gone. All I know is that they're in the game. That much I can tell."

"I guess that means he didn't kill the Demingtons," Pu said.

The nervous feeling in my gut increased.

Would he have done that? Really? Could he still do that?

"Archie, can you tell where he is?" George asked.

"No," Archie said and sighed.

"What do we do now?" Pu asked. "Try to hunt him down?"

"I think this just means we have to keep playing the game to get to the end of it ASAP," Archie replied. "We need Sylvie."

"Fine, fine. We'll keep playing the game. But we have to get rid of that psycho somehow before he duct tapes my mouth shut again," Pu said.

"Then roll the dice, furball," George said as he threw the dice at Pu.

After some swearing, Pu rolled the dice. Landing on 5, a space with a goose image on it, he was told to move ahead another 5 spaces. Then it was Archie's turn to roll. While Pu asked George why the goose spaces were lucky when George clearly wasn't lucky at all, Archie rolled a 13, which landed him on a space with an X through it. This meant he had to go all the way back to the beginning.

I was next. Already on space 16, I clearly had the advantage to really push us forward. But there was probably more than one X space on a board this size. Rolling a measly two, I landed on a goose. Which moved me forward two more spaces. Onto....

"The Bridge!!!" George announced, opening his wings. "Please keep your hands, arms, legs, and feet inside the vehicle at all times while you enjoy being zapped to The Bridge!"

# CHAPTER TEN.

*But First, The Cave.*

*By Morrow.*

The night managed to pass by without any great event.

Lontano snored and slept and snored and slept. He never sprang from the bed to see what was the matter, i.e. how three little girls with mysterious abilities were watching him sleep in shifts.

Exactly nine hours after he had gone to sleep we poked him awake with the room's fire iron. He promptly inquired about breakfast, which was, luckily, available downstairs. After our tasty and filling food, the six of us went off on our journey to the cave on foot, despite Lontano's protestations that we should just magically transfer ourselves there. My sisters and I wouldn't agree to it, as it was unpredictable in our current predicament. We needed to keep a close eye on him.

And cementing that feeling of dread—of what he may or may not be plotting against us—was the fact that throughout the night, and during breakfast, and on our walk, I felt as if we were being watched. I cast a surveillance spell, which would alert me of any threatening auras nearby. But it found nothing.

"I did the same thing," Nora whispered to me as we walked. "I got zilch."

"What do you think it is?" I asked.

"Maybe just something in the game that watches us?" she whispered.

"But I haven't felt its presence the whole time we've been in here though," I said.

Curiosity unsatisfied and uneasiness increased, we arrived at the cave. This was a good thing because I believe we were all pretty tired of listening to Lontano complain about having to walk more, after having to walk yesterday. Oh, the humanity.

"Why noodle?!?! Why have you betrayed me so???" we heard someone inside exclaim.

Lontano excitedly followed Ellie into the

cave, looking for some furniture to apply himself to. The large cavern was laid out as a modern home with an open floor plan, one section of which was a huge, messy kitchen. An old man was standing there in his undershirt and boxer shorts, yelling at a ramen noodle that had fallen onto the floor.

"Why couldn't it have been a young, hot ghost of Michelangelo in his underwear?" Ellie whispered to Nora and me.

"Who are you people? Oh god, not you idiots," the old, not-hot ghost of Michelangelo said to the two moldwarps, as he rolled his eyes.

"It's good to see you again, too, Mikey," Puggy said, smiling.

"We're here to see if your shipment of Japanese snacks came in," Perdita added, settling himself into the lounge chair by the TV. "You always get the best stuff."

"Of course I do. But this isn't a convenience store. I don't stock them for you. And it's not my fault that you two can't conjure up wasabi chips any better than you can paint," Mikey said. "Go home. You know I don't like people. Go home."

"Well, we're not here for *just* your snacks. So there's no need to get nasty. We're also here to possibly assist these four, who are playing the Game of Goose," Puggy said.

Michelangelo stopped slurping up his noodles, and looked at each of our faces.

"A psychopathic demi-god and three imps? Why are you four playing the game?" he asked.

"I'm a god. Not a demi-god. Also, this game-playing is not by choice," Lontano said, and sighed. "What task would you like us to accomplish for you? Oh, Ghost of the Well—ooooooo!"

His sarcasm game was strong today. Almost as strong as his fake ghost noises game.

"I want you to go home. As I said two seconds ago, I don't like people. Go."

"We could clean your house for you," Ellie suggested. "This place is a sty."

There was a ton of empty, old, rotting take-out containers scattered around the place, as well as a healthy layer of dirty laundry, dust, and crumbs over most of the furniture and floor.

"Well, my dried-up-turd-of-a-maid was a dried-up-turd-of-a-maid who couldn't do the work without bothering me. So I had to fire her. But I doubt you people would do any better. You're just children, and that '*god*' Lontano isn't going to do jack for any task. Wait, wait, hold on."

Michelangelo grabbed his bowl of ramen noodles and walked over to my sisters and me in order to—I'm not exactly sure—examine us?

"You're just children," he repeated. "That would mean you might know about, well—a game I play. Children usually know about these things."

"Ugh. Not that crap," Lontano whined.

"You already know what I'm going to ask you about?" Mikey asked. "When did you become psychic as well as psychotic, Lontano?"

"Mother Shipton told us you'd want to win in a video game," Lontano said. "She's the psychic one."

"Ah, that girl. She and her team have been beating mine in all of the server rankings. Left and right. I need to defeat that wench."

"So you know she's been playing?" I asked.

"Of course. Her avatar showed up twenty minutes after she and I had a huge argument about me staying here without her permission, and she knows I play that game. Then that avatar proceeded to challenge me in every aspect of the gameplay: overall rankings, player versus player, team combat, dungeon raids. You name it, she's beaten me. Do you think I'm dumb? Do you think I have birds for brains? Of course it's her. And she's vicious and unforgiving. So I have to beat her and put her in her place."

"Uh, unfortunately, just because we're children doesn't mean we know how to play video games," Nora interrupted him. "We were shut-ins, but not that kind of shut-in."

"But I want you guys to help me beat her team," he replied. "Clearly that's how you could be useful to me. Other than that, you're useless and should go."

"We're not useless. We make a mean chocolate babka," Nora replied. "How about that instead? A Dobos torta? Or something savory? Bacon, chive, and cheddar scones?"

"I can magically procure any food I want from the best chefs in the world. I am the ghost of Michelangelo after all. Why would I need you to bake for me?"

"Good point," Nora said.

"I need you to beat Mother Shipton and her team. There. Your task is set. Go on. If you aren't going to do that, leave me alone."

"Where's the snacks?" Puggy asked. "We can at least eat while these girls think."

"Stay away from my snacks you dirty idle-headed pig-boar," Mikey answered.

"I blame you and your constant insults for my binge-eating tendencies," Puggy replied.

"Should I compose a sonnet for you?" Mikey asked. "Its subject will be you leaving my house as quickly as possible."

As they argued about eating Michelangelo's snacks, Lontano napped on the sofa, and my sisters and I discussed our most pressing issue, amongst many.

"I've only read about this type of MMORPG thing," Ellie whispered to Nora and me. "I've never played one."

"Can we cast a spell to give ourselves the knowledge and skills necessary to beat Mother Shipton?" Nora asked.

"That seems a little bit different than anything we've tried before," I replied. "Video Game Spells 101 wasn't exactly on our course schedule with Eagle."

Meanwhile, Puggy and Perdita had discovered the aforementioned box of snacks hidden in the kitchen, and after swearing at them some more Michelangelo gave up and left them to eat. Then he led my sisters and me over to his computer.

"I play this game a lot," he said. "Okay, I play it all day. And all night. I don't really do anything else anymore. I have so many unfinished projects I was working on, but now this is just all-consuming. If I didn't feel the need to beat this girl, I might actually be able to get on with my life."

Which was an odd thing for a ghost to say.

Where exactly was his life going?

He sat down in his desk chair, put his headset on, fired up the game, and began playing it like a professional gamer. Eyes glued to the screen. Right hand glued to the mouse. Left hand glued to the keyboard. He explained things to us as his avatar moved around and performed mysterious actions. But he might as well have been speaking in Swahili for all I knew.

Fifteen or so painful minutes passed of Michelangelo's excited MMORPG explanation-ing to three girls who nodded, and nodded, and nodded —but looked very lost.

"If there was background music right now it would be the kind that plays in a horror movie while a serial killer chokes a cheerleader to death and you see the life drain from her face as she struggles," Nora whispered to Ellie and me. "That kind of high-pitched violin squealing that makes your blood run cold. I'm going to see my life flash before my eyes soon."

"What are we supposed to do?" I asked. "I can't even follow what he's saying to us or doing in the game."

"I've been trying to take mental notes, but I'm lost, too," Ellie said. "Like that thing he just clicked on, why would he do that? And why did he just put that thing over there? What's he doing now?"

"*Uuuuhggghhhhhhhhhaaarrrggghhh,*" Lontano half-screamed, half-gurgled from the sofa, where he'd been peacefully snoring. "I can't stand this anymore. Talking. Talking. Talking. I can't sleep with all this talking! Which server are you on? What's your username, level, team members? I missed those parts because I was trying to sleep."

Michelangelo turned to stare at him in disbelief, but didn't answer.

"Fine, fine, fine," Lontano said, snapping his fingers and magically producing another desk, chair, and computer for himself, across from Michelangelo's. "I'll figure it out on my own."

He sat down at the computer, turned it on, and put on a headset. Then a game chat window popped up on Michelangelo's screen.

"*ForbiddenWarrior wants to join my team?!?!?*" Michelangelo exclaimed. "That's you?!?!?!"

"I see you also have King Charles I on your team, and Pope Julius II. Still room for me," Lontano said. "Send me a team request."

Michelangelo stood up and stared at Lontano, who kept his eyes on his computer screen.

"*ForbiddenWarrior?!* That's really you? That's the legendary highest-ranked player on this server. Did you just hack into someone's account???" Michelangelo asked.

"No, I didn't just hack someone's account. That's me. Now send me that team request."

"Forbidden Warrior? That's your username?" Nora asked. "Psshhh. How'd you come up with that? A comic book? A bad martial arts movie?"

"Um, uh. It's a long story. But my sister came up with it," Lontano answered, unconvincingly.

"ForbiddenWarrior has logged over 500 days of play since this game's beta release," Michelangelo said, still in an incredulous tone. "That can't possibly be you. You'd have spent every hour of your life doing this instead of being a weirdo out there doing weird things, which we all know you've been doing."

"I may have been a weirdo doing weird things *inside* this game," Lontano replied. "Or I may not have been. Who knows. Now send me that damn team request before I pick up this computer monitor and smash it over your head."

Michelangelo sat back down and seemed to comply with Lontano's order. Things happened on the computer screen. So that meant they were playing, right?

"Your equipment is lacking. No wonder you can never beat her. And none of your team members are ranked higher than her team members. How'd you expect to beat her? I'll start sharing my equipment stash with you guys. And I think we need to do some big quests and boss fights first to level up Charles and Guiliano a bit more, as well," Lontano explained. "You're just in no shape to beat her as you are now."

Michelangelo glared at Lontano, who didn't even notice. But they continued to strategize and move forward with one plan after another toward the goal of—of what? Making Mother Shipton pay for being a better player than Michelangelo? Seems a bit dumb. Just let her kick your butt old man, and live your afterlife knowing there are some battles you can't win, right?

"I'm not sure if Lontano's proficiency with this game is a good sign or a bad sign," Ellie whispered to Nora and me.

"What do you mean?" I asked.

"Well, does being the legendary highest-ranked player on a server increase or decrease your chances of being completely nuts?" she asked.

"I'm just curious about how everyone we meet seems to know who he is, but yet not really know who he is—you get me?" Nora asked.

"I get you," I said. "Like they smile, shake his hand, and eat dinner together, but they're clearly scared of him, Forbidden Warrior or not."

Then Nora tilted her chin toward Puggy and Perdita, who were now furiously drinking glasses of milk after trying extra hot curry potato sticks. Then they sat down at the kitchen table, but mostly draped themselves across it, struggling not to cry. Taking Nora's chin-tilting-cue, we made our way over to the table and joined them.

"So how do you guys know Lontano?" Ellie opened up the conversation.

Perdita coughed and cried for several moments before responding.

"Don't eat these," he said as he pointed at the bag of sticks. "They're horrible and I want to die."

"Aren't you already dead?" Nora asked.

"Well, I want to die again."

"Is that possible? Uh, never mind. So—again—how do you guys know Lontano?" Ellie asked.

"We met him back in, when was that? Well, I think I met him before you, right?" Perdita asked Puggy.

"Of course you did, you dolt, you died before me. You were a ghost years before I became one," Puggy answered, also coughing his response, in between gulps of milk.

"Why does being a ghost matter?" I asked.

"Well, usually you only meet Gods of Death when you die, right?" Puggy asked.

"I guess that's true," I answered.

Although I didn't really have a clue about that.

"So he's a God of Death?" Ellie asked.

"A Demi-God of Death, and now half of a God of Destruction. Although even that seems a bit tenuous, reading his erratic aura," Perdita said.

"And he's responsible for making people into ghosts?" Nora asked.

"Well, once upon a time he helped Riot with

that. She's a God of Death. But now he doesn't do much of that anymore. Too busy going insane. Probably all those lost ghosts driving him batty somehow," Puggy said. "And of course no one's seen Riot in quite awhile. So he may be shouldering that burden on his own."

"Lost ghosts?" I asked.

"There's hundreds of 'em," Perdita said. "Maybe thousands? Millions? Who knows? They're lost, so there isn't a way to tally them up. People died, sure, probably. But their ghosts never showed up in the Realm of the Dead. Never joined us. Never went anywhere. So where are they?"

"No one knows?" Ellie asked.

"Well, the rumors say Riot and Ischia knew, and of course Tiziano—I mean—Lontano. They had something to do with it. But it's all rumors. No facts to go on," Puggy explained. "And those rumors only came along long after it seemed to stop."

"So there are no more lost ghosts?" Nora asked.

"Well, no new ones at least," Perdita said. "But it was all lejerdemani. Only us. Only the magical people. So, of course, that's really suspicious, right? Why just us?"

"It's all really suspicious," Puggy added. "Don't trust him. He may be charming as all heck, but don't trust him."

"Don't worry," I said. "We don't."

Of course Lontano had basically said that we shouldn't trust these two men either. But we could still use them for reconnaissance purposes. Whether they knew or said the truth or not.

"Do all lejerdemani become ghosts when they die?" I asked. "We, um, don't encounter a lot of ghosts where we're from."

"Where would that be?" Puggy asked. "Must be someplace truly astounding if it's not crawling with ghosts. Everyone—well, almost everyone —can become a ghost when they die. Lejerdemani or normal human. Only heinous criminals are destined for something different."

"So most ghosts go around visiting their relatives that are still alive, right?" I asked.

"The recently dead? Sure. But people like Puggy and myself, well, everyone we knew when we were alive is dead now, too. So we're all ghosts together. Most of us anyway," Perdita explained.

"But there's one caveat," Puggy added. "If those

ghosts didn't like those relatives, they certainly wouldn't visit them, right? You wouldn't hang around people you don't like, right? Or maybe you *would* hang around people you don't like to harass them? I guess that all depends on your own attitude. But yes, contact between the dead and the undead is normal, but only lejerdemani can see ghosts, and not even all lejerdemani. Regular humans can't see them."

Well, we certainly weren't regular humans.

So why couldn't my sisters and I ever see the ghosts of our parents?

Or at least our mother.

She was a lejerdemani.

"You guys must be brand-new gods if you don't know about all of this," Puggy said. "Did you forget to attend the seminars or something? There's a reason why you're supposed to go to school, so you don't lower yourself to asking ghosts these types of questions."

"We're not above asking questions," Ellie replied, smirking at him. "Only really stupid people don't ask questions. And the small one is just really curious about everything, all the time."

Was I the 'small one'?

Should I be insulted?

"So just to satisfy *my curiosity*," I interrupted her. "Let's craft a scenario. Let's say your parents were lejerdemani, but they never visited you after they died, as ghosts. What does that mean?"

Ellie and Nora looked at me with an intensity that suggested they might not want to hear the answer to that question.

But I felt the need to ask it.

"Well, as you can guess from what we just said, it's probably one of three things," Perdita said. "One: They were heinous criminals, unworthy of ghosthood. Two: They're two of the lost ghosts, and who the heck knows what happened to them. Three: They didn't like their kid, and didn't want to see 'em anymore."

"So there's no ghost amnesia spell where someone casts it on them and they forget who they are and can't remember the fact that they had kids?" Nora asked. "And that would be the reason why they never showed up?"

"Ghost amnesia spell? Never heard of that," Puggy said. "I guess it would have its uses, but I'm not sure what they'd be."

"It's probably Sven's fault," Nora whispered to

Ellie and me, as we got up from the table, and left Puggy and Perdita to their glasses of milk. "He wouldn't let them in to see us."

Perhaps that was a sound argument, but it was unconvincing. Why would a magical force field meant to protect us also keep us from seeing the ghosts of our parents?

The most disappointing part of this conversation was my realization that Eagle and Penny must have known that ghosts exist, and probably knew why our parents' ghosts never showed up at our front door, and yet never shared that information with us.

Or had their ghosts been there all along and we three numbskulls just couldn't see them? But we can see these guys. Or is that only because we're in the Game of Goose? Gosh, this is frustrating. There were so many things I wanted to ask Eagle, or Penny, or just someone trustworthy.

"Maybe they were never ghosts in the first place, for some reason," Ellie suggested.

"Do you think we should ask Lontano about it?" Nora pondered. "Or at least about the lost ghosts?"

"Should we really reveal to him that we're interested in that kind of thing?" I asked. "He may use it against us somehow."

"Well, if he has hearing like Eagle's then he already knows what we've talked about," Nora said.

"Yeesh. This is really annoying," Ellie said. "Why can't he just be a normal guy and I can just enjoy staring at him? Instead I'm wondering about all the ways he's trying to come up with to kill us."

Meanwhile, a screaming match had broken out over at the computers.

Michelangelo and Lontano were swearing at each other with vehemence, each accusing the other of game misconduct. Clearly there was a problem with two highly competitive people coexisting peacefully on the same team. Even when they were meant to be looking out toward the enemy at the gate, they still spent most of their time trying to prove their own superiority.

"Why do I feel like this was doomed from the get-go?" Ellie asked Nora and me, quietly, as we walked back toward the epicenter of violent words.

"*Oy!* Just *what* do you think you're doing?!?!" Mother Shipton yelled from the entryway. "How dare you recruit ForbiddenWarrior to your team!!! Did you hack his account or something? That's just low, Mikey, even for you."

"I didn't hack his account. It's this jerk," Mikey said, pointing at that jerk Lontano.

"I hope you enjoyed being completely destroyed, my dear," Lontano said, smiling.

"You're ForbiddenWarrior?" she asked.

"Yes, and let's not go through all that again," he replied, and sighed.

"Fine, fine. Let's pretend you are. Mikey's team is ranked higher than mine now, so he has to teach me how to draw," she said.

"What? I have to what?" Mikey asked.

"I told them where you live in exchange for them getting you to teach me how to draw."

"Well, I wasn't part of that deal, so I'm not going to do anything," he said.

"Alright, then I'm going to recruit Forbidden-Warrior to my team and win back my superior rankings," she replied.

"No, no, no, no. No," Mikey said. "That's not possible."

"Then teach me how to draw. I have a fanfic I'm writing, and I want illustrations to go with it."

"I'll do no such thing. Why would I degrade myself in such a way?"

Mother Shipton and Michelangelo stared—or rather glared at each other—having reached an impasse in the conversation/argument.

"Those two moldwarps probably know how to draw," Nora offered, pointing at Puggy and Perdita. "They're painters or something. Even though they just look like milk-addicts right now. Maybe they can teach you."

"They can draw?" she asked. "Fine, I'll ask them to teach me."

Mother Shipton stuck out her tongue at Michelangelo, and then made a beeline to the kitchen table. But Michelangelo quickly got up from his desk and intercepted her approach.

"No. Don't ask them," he said. "They're perverts. Like truly, complete perverts. I'll do it."

"You'll teach me how to draw?"

"Yes. I agree to this nonsense. But never ask me for anything else ever again."

"You're awfully full of yourself for someone who's squatting on my property like a vagrant," she said.

"Do you want my help or not?" he asked. "Let me give these idiots their work of art so they can go back to the game board and get out of my hair, and then we can get started."

"Are you calling *me* an idiot, after I just helped you?" Lontano asked.

"I only speak the truth," Mikey replied as he snapped his fingers and a massive stone statue of some muscular naked dude appeared in front of him.

It was easily eight feet tall, with a bronze lion skin draped near his hip (but not hiding anything), and a large club under his right arm that he leaned against as if it were a crutch.

Michelangelo touched the tip of his finger onto the tip of the statue's finger and it—or he—came alive. He yawned and stretched, and then clapped Michelangelo on the shoulder.

"Long time no see, buddy. Why'd you call me up?" the statue guy asked.

"I'm giving you to these weirdos," Mikey said as he pointed at my sisters and me. "Try not to hate me too much for this."

The statue looked at us.

We looked at the statue.

He shrugged.

We shrugged.

And we were back at the game board, where the goose was seated on the red couch, reading.

"The Lost Hercules. Interesting," George said.

"I guess you must've met Michelangelo."

After having noticed Ellie staring at all of his naked body parts like an agog pervert, Hercules tied the lion skin around his waist. It moved and draped like a real lion skin, even though it was made of bronze.

"That wasn't necessary," Ellie said.

"I'm pretty sure it was," he replied. "So who are you guys? A God of Death—or something? And three fairies?"

"That's not really important," Lontano said. "So goose—what just happened and how can we get to Archie?"

"I have no idea what happened. You tell me."

"We were sucked into the stupid game to Mother Shipton's stupid Well, or rather a version of it from a poster. And we did a stupid task and got this stupid statue," Lontano rattled on. "Why did that happen?"

"I don't know," George said. "I assume it's just your bizarre bond with Archie that's triggering this. You're not rolling any dice, so I can't tell you what happened or how."

Lontano scowled at the goose, and the goose scowled back.

And then we were outside a pub.

"Switzerland!!!" Lontano yelled. "*Ssswww-whhhhh!!!*"

"Basel to be precise," a man seated at a nearby table explained. "You're inside a 16th century map of the city, though. So don't get too excited. We don't even have chocolate shops yet."

Lontano answered him with a string of Italian curse words.

"I guess you *aren't* that excited," the man replied. "Or maybe you really wanted to go to the chocolate shops."

A woman came out of the pub and delivered a drink to the man.

"Welcome to Zur Blume, our inn. How can I help you this afternoon? Do you need a room, a meal, or both?" she asked us.

"I need all three, and a lejerdemani ghost," Lontano said.

"Hmmm. Alright," the woman replied. "Those are Holbein's legs painted up there on the inn's side wall, hanging down from the scaffolding. He's supposed to be painting the wall, but he's off doing god-knows-what. Thinks the legs'll fool me. Ingrate. I'm sure he'll be back for dinner soon though. And the quiz night. C'mon in and I'll get you a room key and some food."

"Holbein?" I asked Ellie as we followed the woman into the inn.

"Hans, the Younger Holbein, most likely. A Northern Renaissance painter and printmaker," she answered.

"And yet another pain in the butt. I wonder what god-awful task he'll want us to accomplish," Lontano said. "Though I see little point in doing these tasks since when we finish one we're immediately bounced to another location, but not anywhere near Archie. Wait, lady— you haven't see the Jainkohiltzaile, a cat, and the old God of Destruction have you?"

"No. Are they playing the game, too?" she asked.

Everyone seemed to know all about this game. Everyone but us.

"Yes, they are. Probably," Lontano said.

"Nope. Haven't had anybody here playing the game in a very long time."

"God, then what's the point of this?" Lontano whined. "I just want to kill Archie. Is that possible?"

"You guys wanna get out of the game?" she asked.

"Yes, that would be lovely," Lontano said.

"But isn't it true that you can't get out of the Game of Goose until you win it?" the woman asked.

"True," Lontano answered. "Wait, is that true? I'm not sure."

"So we keep playing until we win?" I asked. "And then we'll automatically leave?"

"But how do we even know if us playing it counts?" Lontano asked. "Again, we aren't even rolling any dice."

"Do you think we'll be stuck in the game forever?!" I asked, fearful.

"Ugh. I'll eventually figure a way out of this," Lontano said, and sighed, as he sat down at the table the woman directed us to.

"The freckled one has the Wynne brush. I'm not sure why you're worried," Hercules said. "She can just write out that she wants all of us to leave the game."

"The Wynne brush?" I asked.

"Yeah, it's in the back pocket of her pants," Hercules replied, pointing at Nora's butt. Well, her pocket really. Which was next to her butt.

"This thing?" she asked as she lifted a black-handled paintbrush out of her pocket.

"Yeah, it's quite the powerful object. Didn't

you know?" Hercules asked.

"No. I stole it off a desk at a school's library," she replied. "I didn't know it was special."

"*Dear god,*" I said. "Why can't you ever keep your hands to yourself?"

She winked at me.

"So how's it work?" she asked Hercules.

"You write down what you want in charcoal on a piece of parchment and then wipe the words away with the brush. It's useful for wishes. But it only works for positive things. So it's not like you can wish for—say—Michelangelo—to have diarrhea for a month. That wouldn't work," Hercules explained.

"Huh, who knew?" Nora said.

"It's a very famous lejerdemani artifact," Hercules added. "I'm surprised you guys don't know about it."

"They aren't very educated about the lejerdemani," Lontano said. "Goddesses of Mischief or something who have lived under a rock their whole lives. Don't mind their stupidity."

Lontano snapped his fingers and magically produced a stick of drawing charcoal and a piece of parchment.

"Write down 'we want to be with Archie' on

here," he said as he handed the supplies to Nora.

"Why me?" she asked.

"Well, we can try you, and then another one of you girls. It works best for women. Not so well with men," Hercules explained. "I don't think you have to be a lejerdemani. So let's just see what we can do."

Nora did as instructed, and after the words were complete she feverishly rubbed away at them with the brush. Nothing happened.

I tried. Ellie tried. Nothing happened. Hercules tried. Lontano tried. And nothing happened.

The words were erased. Many times. But we weren't with Archie.

"Alright, alright. Clearly the author doesn't want us to easily use this as a tool to get out of the game," Lontano said.

"Maybe it's because you being with Archie isn't really a positive wish," Ellie said.

"Why wouldn't it be? Obviously I love and adore him," Lontano said in a dry tone.

A server appeared with plates of sliced meats, breads, cheeses, and roasted vegetables, which were laid out in front of us.

"Lydia says you're looking for a lejerdemani ghost for the game," a young man said as he joined us at our table.

"Holbein?" Ellie asked.

"That's me," he said, smiling.

"When you said Holbein the Younger, you weren't kidding," Nora said to Ellie. "This guy's just a kid."

"I'm 18. Give or take a few years," he replied. "Why would I go around as some old, balding ghost dude?"

"Good point," Nora replied. "Also, I feel a strong sense of déjà vu."

"How's Michelangelo these days, Herc?" Holbein asked our statuesque friend.

"Annoying. Per usual," he replied. "Why even ask? You can see my situation."

"So what kind of task do you need us to accomplish?" Nora asked Holbein.

"Can it be something where Hercules shows off his muscles?" Ellie asked. "Like lifting something really heavy, repeatedly, in the sunshine, his skin glistening...."

"Stop it," I interrupted her.

"I want to win the inn's quiz tonight," Holbein said. "So I'm afraid it'll be more of a workout for the brain than the body."

"What's with you people and winning? You

have to win at everything. Not everyone can win all the time, ya know? There has to be losers. You waste your afterlives playing games," Lontano said. "Don't you have anything better to do?"

"Aren't you the one who's spent 500 days playing that video game? Forbidden Warrior?" Nora asked.

"And aren't you people playing the Game of Goose right now?" Holbein asked. "I think that's also a game. The word 'game' *is* in the name."

"Let's move on," Lontano said.

"So for this quiz night," Ellie said. "What are the question categories?"

"They don't announce them until the game starts," Holbein answered. "But we have to win. No matter what. Henry VIII kicked me off his team last week because I got a question wrong. One question. Ungrateful idiot. Who does he think he is?"

"Probably thinks of himself as a dead King of England," Hercules said. "They're usually pretty full of themselves."

"What kinds of question categories have there been in the past?" Ellie asked.

"Last week it was English Counties, Famous Elizabeths, 90s Pop Music, and the History of

Cricket," Holbein said.

"Oh. *God*," Lontano said as he purposefully smacked his forehead down onto the table and left his head there. He may have started crying. I'm not sure.

"Oh, ho, oh," a young man fake-laughed at us as he walked over to our table. "Is this *your team* for tonight's quiz?"

"No, not necessarily," Holbein answered.

"I sure hope not if you intend on winning," the man said, smirking.

"Friends, this is Henry VIII," Holbein explained, rolling his eyes.

"And I'm also the winner of tonight's quiz," Henry added. "You can call me Hal, by the way."

"Don't you think it's a bit premature to call yourself the winner when it hasn't even started yet?" Hercules asked.

"Oh, like a gigantic statue is going to beat me? Hercules, you're known for your strength, not your brains," Hal replied.

"I have both, thank you very much," Hercules said.

"Well, *I'm* not participating in this quiz night," Lontano interrupted. "It's too stupid."

"You're probably only saying that because you

know you won't know any of the answers," Hal said. "And you don't want to look dumb in front of your three young wives here."

"No. Wait, no," Lontano replied. "One: I'd never look dumb. It's physically impossible. Two: These aren't my wives—they're my enemies. Although in most marriages I guess that's the same thing. Three: I don't want to participate because, because, well—I'd rather start singing an emotional love ballad with this whole pub until I want to rip my own ears off."

"What's wrong with group singing?" Hercules asked.

"Nothing, nothing," Lontano answered, rubbing his forehead. "But there's a reason why I avoid karaoke nights."

"I can see that I have nothing to worry about," Hal said, and smiled with satisfaction. "You're all morons. Holbein, you'll never win."

Then he gave a little wave and walked away.

We looked at each other. Perhaps expecting something miraculous to happen, while individually pondering how in the world we would ever win a quiz night.

"I know a lot of useless information. And I mean *a lot* of useless information. But it's not like I was prepping for a trivia game," Ellie said. "I don't think we can do this."

"Well, if it's not with you guys, how can I win the quiz tonight?" Holbein asked. "I don't have other options. There aren't droves of trivia masters just wandering into this map."

"Use the Wynne brush," Hercules suggested. "Call up a winning team."

Nora grabbed the parchment and charcoal, scrawled out 'bring us a winning trivia game team,' and then promptly erased the words with the brush.

Six women materialized before us. And a loud gasp came from the other side of the pub— the direction that Hal had walked toward. He quickly popped into view and scrambled over to our table to approach the women.

"*What are you doing here?!?!*" he asked. "I thought you were on a spa holiday! *AND* we agreed that you'd never set foot in this map. This was supposed to be my place, *MY PLACE*."

"Well, if you stop whining long enough for us to speak, we'd explain it to you," the tallest woman said, while glaring at Hal. "The Wynne brush just called us here, to this seventh circle of Hell where you live."

"Arrrggghhh, no Holbein!" Hal spat, and slapped him on the shoulder. "You can't use them as your team!"

"Why not? I think a team composed of your wives' ghosts is very appropriate. We will be the ideal group to defeat you," Holbein said.

"Speaking of being dead, Hal," the red-haired woman said. "Why are you going around as a healthy young man when you're really a fat, disgusting, pus-covered, ulcerous bag of guts?"

"I once looked like this, too," he answered. "I wasn't always overweight and diseased!"

"Well, at least you know you were grotesque," she replied.

"It was just my legs! Oh, never mind. Anyway, *they* can't compete here. They have to go back to where they were," Hal said.

"Why? Are you too scared that we'll win?" the shortest woman asked.

"You won't win," Hal replied.

"Then there shouldn't be a problem with us participating," the darkest-haired woman said.

"You're tricking me. I know you're tricking me. And it won't work. Go back to the spa resort and leave me alone," Hal said.

"At least you're aware of it," the darkest-haired

woman answered. "But, honestly, if you aren't confident enough to beat us in a silly trivia game, then can you really even show up to compete?"

"*Aaaagggghhhh*," Hal cried out and then stomped off back to his table on the other side of the pub.

"Well, this should be fun," the woman with the sharp nose said, smiling.

# CHAPTER ELEVEN.

*The Bridge, aka A Very Fry Orgy.*

*By Stella Exchequer Grum.*

(Maple: I was trying to write this section with a voice-to-notes app while laying down in bed like a lazy lump of flesh and I said something—I don't even know what—and the phone thought I said: "A Very Fry Orgy." That was certainly *not* what I had said, but I decided I needed to keep that as the subtitle to this part.

Stella: Wow. That's deep.

Maple: It is deep. It is. It means nothing. And everything. Simultaneously.

Stella: And have you now decided to make my middle name Exchequer?

Maple: Maybe. I'm not sure yet. Then your initials would be SEG. And then this would be an excellent SEGue into the next section.

Stella: Groan.)


The Bridge we were zapped to was a small red footbridge that arched dramatically over a little pond surrounded by trellises brimming with purple wisteria flowers.

We were clearly in Japan, or something like Japan. It certainly looked like the Japanese-style gardens I had once visited in San Francisco. On a field trip. In high school. With my father.

A young man was leaning on the bridge railing, studying the scene intently when we arrived.

"Raphael!" Archie said as he stepped forward to shake the man's hand.

"Long time no see!" the man said as he returned Archie's handshake enthusiastically.

"This is Stella and Pu," Archie gestured to us. "This is Raphael."

"It's nice to meet you, Stella," Raphael said as he smiled and offered me his hand.

I automatically reached for it like polite people do, forgetting I'm not supposed to touch any man, ever. Archie quickly leaned in between us and my hand touched his arm and Raphael's hand simultaneously.

Then things became hazy.

# CHAPTER TWELVE.

*Don't Touch Stella, Ever.*

*Presented by Archie.*

Yeah, it's back to me already. My bad. And we had just started a new chapter. Now this looks unprofessional.

I shouldn't have stepped into Stella's hand, but I really didn't want her to touch Raphael and then transfer Pu's spell to him. Raphael doesn't really need any encouragement in that department. So now I guess it's up to me to tell you what happened after Stella touched my arm. Because she was no longer of sound enough mind to tell this tale.

"Agh, don't touch her, Raph! She's, uh, got leprosy," I said, pushing his hand away.

"*I have leprosy?!?!*" she gasped as she reached for my hand, clasping it firmly. A bad sign.

"No! Ugh. Dammit," I said. "No, you don't actually."

"Free Hugs!!!" she announced as she turned to Raphael, smiling at him ecstatically, and opening her arms wide.

"Whoa alright, my dear," he said, stepping toward her.

"No, no, no," I said as I stepped between them.

"Do you want *your* free hug?" she asked me.

"Oh!" Pu said and laughed, joyously. "I think the spell is working for both of you!"

"What's happening?" Raphael asked, smiling as Stella playfully reached for him.

"She's under a spell," I answered. "But just ignore it."

"No, he should know everything about it!" Pu insisted. "After all, it's one of my more creative spells! She acts bonkers every time she touches a man."

"Any man?" Raphael asked, a glint in his eye. "So even me?"

"Oh! Oh! A pond! Let's go swimming!!!" Stella said to Raphael, as she used her free hand to take his. I should have grabbed both of her hands, dammit.

She dragged us off the bridge to the edge of the pond.

Where she began taking off her shoes.

"*Ayyyyyeeee!!!*" I yelled. "It's a shrine. *Shrine.* They don't allow swimming. It's a sacred place."

"Awwww," she whined.

"Plus that pond is full of biting turtles and gross algae, my dear. I tell you what—I live at a bathhouse. And they have a *mixed* bath. We can go there together," Raphael said, beckoning her with his finger. "Right now."

"Oooooo," Stella cooed as she stepped even closer to Raphael. "Let's go."

"No, no, no. We aren't doing that," I said as I pried Raphael's hand off of hers. I was now effect-ively holding his hand instead.

Pu had lost it and was literally peeing himself with laughter on the bridge. He wasn't going to be helpful at all, was he?

"Gosh, look at how red your ears are, Archie. Are you angry, embarrassed, or something else?" Raphael asked.

"Please don't do that," I said.

"What?" he replied, smiling broadly.

"Let's go to the bathhouse!" Stella sang, swinging my arm.

"I don't think that's a good idea," I replied.

"Okay, then let's play tag! First one to catch me wins!" she squealed as she let go of my hand and bolted across the garden.

Without any shoes on.

Her farting unicorn socks were going to be ruined. Not that I noticed what she was wearing. Cough.

Then she started randomly singing about 'sweets, love, and sunshine' as she darted on and off pathways, over rocks, through bushes.

"Your charms are increasing, my dear!" Raphael shouted as he grinned.

"Don't encourage this," I said.

"Why not? She's fun."

"She's gonna cut her feet open."

"Well, we could always go to my place," Raphael said and winked. "She wanted to go."

Ugh. That.

"Fine, we'll go to the bathhouse!" I yelled to her. "Just come back and put your shoes on!"

Stella stopped her headlong sprint into Tokyo and ran back to us to put her shoes on. Then we rejoined Pu on the now-damp bridge.

"So this spell, every time she touches a man,

she acts like she's uh, passionately nuts?" Raphael asked.

"Something like that," I replied. "But don't touch her. Just start walking toward your house."

"Why'd you cast such a weird spell on her, Pu?" Raphael asked.

"She brought it on herself. These two were refusing to fall in love, or even act cute together. So I had to step in and make some adjustments," Pu said, nodding.

"*They're supposed to fall in love?!*" Raphael asked, shocked. "Archie doesn't fall in love."

"What do you mean?" Stella asked.

"It's not an emotional ability he possesses," Raphael said.

"We'll see about that," Pu said. "The Goddess of Fate has deemed them to be a couple. It's written, in the stars, so to speak."

"Hmmm. I don't know," Raphael said, shaking his head. "Like I said, Archie's never been in love. Not in the 500 or so years I've known him. But *me* on the other hand, well, I'm very popular."

He beamed at Stella, who grinned back.

"Don't get any stupid ideas," I told him.

"Why not? Stella, you probably know that

Italians are the most romantic people in the history of the planet," Raphael said as he reached out to touch her arm, but I stepped forward, and put myself in between them.

"Oh, I know," Stella said, nodding her head enthusiastically. "I met Casanova once."

"*You did?!*" Raphael and I asked in unison.

"When? How? What happened?" I asked.

"What happened?" she asked. Then she stepped forward, to whisper in a flirty tone: "Oh, you know, just some stuff."

Some stuff? What stuff?

Then she began singing again.

What the?

"Intriguing," Raphael said. "How about a piggyback ride to my house, Stella?"

"Ooooohhhh! Yes!" she said and clapped, reaching for him again.

"No, I'll do it!" I insisted.

"*You will?!?*" everyone asked in unified surprise.

"I don't know what that is, but I'll do it," I said.

"Okay! Even better!" she said as she raised her fist in the air triumphantly, and then scrambled onto my back.

This is a piggyback ride?!?!

She banged her chin against the back of my head, accidentally. Several times. And then licked my ear, purposefully. Once.

"Ack!" I squeaked.

Yes, I admit I squeaked.

Pu was laughing even harder now.

If that was possible.

"You see? Archie doesn't fall in love," Raphael assured Pu. "He can't even stand a moist ear."

"Like I said, we'll see about that," Pu huffed.

"Well, besides this very amusing and inventive spell, which I *will* milk later for my own ends as much as possible, what brings you guys to my little corner of the universe?" Raphael asked.

"The Game of Goose," Pu said. "We have to win it, and we landed on 'The Bridge' space. Where are we this time? Japan? Tokyo?"

"Yes. This is a woodcut print of the Kameido Tenjin shrine in Tokyo. I live here part of the year to see the wisteria in bloom. But uh, for science, how long does she act like that after she touches a man?" Raphael asked.

"We aren't sure," Pu said. "She touches a man. Weird stuff goes down. She doesn't remember it. Might last for five minutes, might last for hours. Then she comes back to her senses. Doesn't have a clue what happened in between. It's fantastic."

"No. It's not fantastic. It's the farthest thing from fantastic," I said.

"So how can we make this spell last as long as possible?" Raphael asked.

"Well, it stopped last time when she was hungry. So we just have to keep her well-fed, and you never know how long it will last," Pu answered.

"Don't tell him that stuff," I said.

"Why? Are you going to starve me to death until I turn back to normal?" Stella asked.

"No," I replied.

But I kinda wanted to say yes.

Was it cruel to starve her until the spell turned off?

Probably.

Then she started giggling and rubbing her nose against my hair.

That's odd. That's nice.

Oh no.

"Raphael, start walking *really* fast to your house right now and don't even think of taking the long way," I said.

"Oh, definitely not. We need to get there ASAP so Stella can eat!" he answered as he happily skipped forward.

# CHAPTER THIRTEEN.

*The Inn, Continued, aka: Why Lontano Should Always Be Under a Loose Lips Spell.*

*By Morrow.*

The Quizmaster, as she was called, eventually showed up at the inn and announced the evening's question categories.

"Ancient Phoenician Trade Routes," she said.

"Good, good," Hal approved proudly, and loud enough for the whole pub to hear.

"The History and Techniques of Hydroponics," the Quizmaster continued, although she was visibly annoyed that Hal had interrupted her.

"*What?* Fine, fine. We can manage that," Hal said, once again loud enough for people in China to hear him.

"Scientific Breakthroughs of the Space Race," the Quizmaster said, gritting her teeth.

"*That's crap!* Why so much science?!" Hal yelled at her.

"Should we have a world without science? Since it is beneath your Majesty?" the Quizmaster asked him, sarcastically.

"Um, never mind," he replied. "Go on."

"Great Female Artists of the 19th and 20th centuries," she finished her list.

"Oh, no, no, *no*. That's not possible. What's with this week's questions? They're ridiculous. There aren't any great female artists of *any* century! Who would even pay attention to art made by a woman?!" Hal spat.

I blinked hard at that. Unsure I had heard him correctly.

But no. That's what he said.

"He so deserves to be tarred, feathered, and then catapulted off the Westminster Bridge, flung into the rotating London Eye," the darkest-haired Queen commented.

"Too bad he's already dead," the red-haired Queen replied. "It would be so enjoyable to murder him."

"Just because *you* don't know about female artists doesn't mean they aren't important," the Quizmaster explained to Hal.

He glared at her, and then proceeded to grumble more quietly with his teammates about the stupidity and unfairness of the question categories, and of the world, of the universe, etc. etc.

And so began a night of incendiary and abusive bickering, swearing, and screaming that was supposedly a pub quiz night. Fueled by endless drinks, sausages, and spaetzle, the game barely managed to escape turning into a full-on bar brawl.

"Is this family?" I whispered, out loud—by accident—as I watched Hal and his wives participate in a yelling match over the accuracy of an answer about Georgia O'Keeffe.

This was the first time I had ever seen a husband and his wife (er, wives) interact in person. I had often wondered what it would be like to have a mother and father in the traditional sense of the word 'family.' Was it like this?

"I don't think observing Henry VIII and his wives will deliver a good example of a family. Genghis Khan might be a better example of a husband in comparison to Henry," Hercules responded as he smiled and pointed toward a man seated at the bar, who waved and smiled in response to the gesture—obviously an acquaintance of his.

"Does the blame of dysfunction lay *solely* on the shoulders of the husband though?" Lontano stuttered, his face pressed into the tabletop.

He had gorged himself on meats, cheeses, and breads. Probably in an amount equal to his own body weight. What was this? Why was he acting weird? Well, more weird. He moved to shove another sausage into his mouth, but somehow without removing his face from the table.

"All things in moderation, man," Hercules said as he gently tried to pry the sausage from Lontano's hand.

"Killing people," Lontano answered, his grip tightening on the sausage. "Hurting them. Making them suffer. Pain. All of those things—in moderation. Eating, never."

"You must be a *real* hoot at parties," Hercules said as he stood up, lifted and twisted Lontano's arm, and managed to remove the sausage from his hand by just eating it himself.

"*Murder*—in moderation," Lontano whispered.

"Why is he acting even nuttier?" Ellie asked. "Normal people don't eat this much."

"It's probably my fault," Nora confessed.

"*Whyyy???*" I asked, eyeballing her. "What did you do?"

"I cast a 'loose lips sink ships' spell on him earlier. Apparently it just caused him to eat a lot, instead of spilling his secrets."

"You did?!" Lontano asked. "*Why would you do that?!*"

"I figured you probably have a lot of good info stored in your bizarre head. And I don't see much of a point in playing too nice with you."

"A point? *A point?* I see. So you don't respect me either. I'm just someone to step all over. Just like her. Well, I told her. I told her," Lontano mumbled, still face down on the table.

"What did you tell her?" Ellie whispered.

"I said. I said. What did I say? You—you have to make room for love. For love to exist in this world," he sputtered. "If you don't create that opportunity, then hate. Hate will always dominate."

"That's kind of a weird thing for *you* to say, when you just extolled the virtues of killing people," Ellie said. "You seem up to your eye-balls in hatred."

"But I loved her, you see?" he said.

"Loved who?" I asked.

"Her. And she said, she said she didn't and couldn't and wouldn't. And. She took my sister from me, and she said never, and she said Archie. Archie, instead. Can you believe that?" he continued. "And I said. I said—you're like a glistening, clear stream that flowed through putrid sewage pipes before it reached—it reached the base of a pristine mountainside. You're dirty, but it's hidden. Beautiful. But really, really disgusting."

Um.

"And then what did she say to that *completely endearing* love confession?" Hercules asked.

"She said, she said in her prissy tone of voice: 'I'm not sure who you're saying that to, but you should really look in the mirror.' Like a snot. Like a total and complete snot."

"What happened then?" I asked.

"And then. And then. I turned her into a plant."

"You what?" Hercules asked. "Is that some kind of a metaphor?"

"No, I turned her into a plant. Verbena. Ver-

168

vain. Verbena Officinalis. The tears of Isis. Devil's bane. Holy herb. Iron wort. She was in the body of Verbena Coventry when I did it, so it seemed fitting."

"So that was Riot?" I asked.

"Yes. My—the—dreaded Heriotza. Yes."

"Where's that plant now?" Ellie asked.

"Somewhere. Somewhere deep, in my heart," he replied, knocking at his own chest with his fist.

"What does that mean?" Nora asked.

"My heart," he continued. "Yes. That. My heart. All those people I've given a piece of my heart to—a slice here, a chunk there. But my heart wasn't all that big to begin with. So where did I get all those pieces to give away? And what's left? Right now? A shriveled, dead piece of nothingness. Like a heart raisin. That's what's left. I kept giving things away I should've never given away. I should've kept them to myself. Kept it all to myself. Maybe then I'd still be—something. Something. Sane? Maybe. Something. I'd be something. But now all I am is pain."

I stared at him.

My mouth hung open. Just a little bit though.

What do you say to someone after that?

'Don't be pain, you pain in the butt???'

"Ummm, that piteous lament aside, where exactly is this place deep in your heart where that plant is?" Ellie asked.

"Life is a game. A heartbreaking one," he whispered, possibly in response to her, or possibly just to say it out loud.

Then he closed his eyes, started snoring, and gurgled drool onto the table.

"And this is why you can't have an actual conversation with this person, kids," Hercules said, shaking his head. "He's not normal."

"On the contrary, this was quite informative and I should've cast that spell on him earlier," Nora said. "Although I think he just countered it somehow. I don't know why he fell asleep instead of talking more."

"I wonder if we can cast it on him again?" Ellie asked. "Despite being slightly incoherent and emotional he just told us that Riot is a plant somewhere."

"*And* he knows where that 'somewhere' is," Nora added.

"Now we just have to get that out of him, and maybe information on where Penny, Eagle, and Derek are," I said.

"Do you think he also knows what's tailing us?" Hercules asked.

"You know about that, too?" Nora asked.

"Well, it's not so much that I *know*, it's that I've felt something watching us since Michelangelo activated me. But I haven't been able to pinpoint what it is."

"We don't know either. We just know it's there," Nora said.

"Have you ever experienced something like it before?" Ellie asked.

"No. Not many people spend their time secretly following me around," Hercules said.

"I would," Ellie replied, blinking at him rapidly like she was trying to be adorable.

"That's called stalking," I said. "I think, rather, we're being hunted."

Lontano woke up, sat up, and smacked his hand down on the table.

"You want to know what family is? This— this is family," he said as he gestured to all of us seated at the table. "A bizarre, random assortment of weirdos who were thrown together. That's family. This is family."

"You must be a very lonely person," Hercules said.

Lontano glared at him with an air of perturbed perplexity. Then he grabbed the room key off the table, stood up—with difficulty, and tried to walk away. But he couldn't.

"*Uggghhhh*, Tall One! Let's go upstairs and sleep. I'm tired!" he whined at Ellie, the keeper of his footsteps.

So we retreated to our room for the night, as we would be useless in Holbein's ongoing quiz battle. We'd just have to find out the results in the morning.

"How old are you three girls?" Hercules asked as we ascended the stairs to the second floor. "You act quite mature for looking like children."

"We're promiscuous. No, that's not it. Precious? Presumptuous? Prepubescent?" Nora tried to explain.

"Precocious," Ellie interrupted her. "The word is precocious. We're—let's just say we've spent more time interacting with books than with our peers, resulting in slightly skewed behavior on our part. You could ask for further details, but I'm not sure it's anything that can really be elucidated."

"I see," Hercules said, as we watched Lontano settle into his beddy blanket cocoon once again.

While we determined the night watch schedule, Lontano began snoring.

"I can take a shift," Hercules suggested. "Although I'm not sure why we're watching him."

"Who says we aren't watching you, too?" Nora asked.

"I guess I'm also a stranger," he replied. "But he's much stranger than I am. I wouldn't trust him."

"While *we* already know that he's not trustworthy, from a lifetime of experience on that issue, how do *you* know that?" I asked.

"His mind is doing something right now," Hercules said. "I can tell the magical wheels are spinning. Something is happening. But I don't know what it is."

"Do you think it has something to do with whatever's following us? Hunting us?" Ellie asked.

"Maybe. But I'm not sure," Hercules said.

"So what do we do now?" Nora asked. "Do we cast another spell to get him to stop whatever it is he's doing?"

"What if he's just trying to figure out a way out of this game?" I asked.

"What if it's something far less innocent?"

Ellie asked.

"Can you sit on him and crush him to death?" Nora asked Hercules.

"Unfortunately, no. Because he's part god, sort of."

"Aren't you part god, too?" Ellie asked.

"I am, but not that kind of god. I'm still just a work of art. I can crush him, but not to death."

"Can we use the Wynne brush to do something?" I asked. "Like sweep him off the face of the Earth?"

"It only grants specific positive wishes," Hercules answered. "And I don't think sweeping him off the face of the Earth would work. Since we aren't even on Earth."

"Could the brush do something to him? Anything? Can it stop whatever it is he's doing?" Ellie asked.

"I think you'd need to know what he's doing in order for it to work properly," Hercules replied.

"We need Stella," Ellie said. "Or Sylvie. Or someone."

And then we all looked at Lontano, whose leg twitched in his sleep.

If he was even asleep at all.

# CHAPTER FOURTEEN.

*Confessions at a Japanese Bathhouse.*

*By Stella Ichthyocoprolite Grum.*

(Stella: Should I even ask what ickythighsco-bralight means?

Maple: It's probably better if you don't know.

Stella: Well, does it have something to do with donkey butts this time?

Maple: Surprisingly, no. And now your initials are SIG, for this SIGnificant chapter.

Stella: Ugh. Let's move on. Before I look up 'ickythighscobralight' and become even more disappointed with my lot in life.)


Whatever Pu's spell was, its effects were slightly different the second time around, and an uncomfortable level of self-awareness accompanied it. At first, when I touched Archie's arm and Raphael's hand, what happened was all very muddled. Who said what? Who did what? It was like that time in the prison cell: a blur.

But within a few minutes I was much more aware of what was happening and who was responsible for these happenings: mostly me, myself, and I, unfortunately. I could feel, hear, and see what was going on around me. But my rational mind had no control over my behavior. The way I moved, what I said, how I said it, who I touched, whose ear I licked—I had no control over any of it.

Was this how I really wanted to act all the time? Had I been holding this in? Or was this just the spell? I was behaving like the people I had always avoided in school. The overly silly and flirtatious people who, in my mind, always had a flashing red light and sirens blaring around them. 'Warning! Flee their presence. Flee now! As fast as possible!' Was I that starved for affection that I'd become one of them?? Sigh.

As much as I'd like to strike the following events from history, I must admit that they happened. Ugh.

Confession #1: Upon entering Raphael's living quarters....

"I need to go to the bathroom," I declared.

"It's that room over there," Raphael said as he gestured toward a doorway.

"Who wants to go with me?" I asked.

Raphael stepped toward me, intrigued, and a mild scuffle broke out between him and Archie.

Confession #2: While Raphael nursed the earlobe that Archie had pulled on earlier in the mild scuffle....

I burst out of the bathroom, in my bra and undies, and asked where the mixed gender bath was located, demanding specific directions.

(p.s. I really should've worn better undergarments for my kidnapping.)

Confession #3: While Raphael clutched the bruised shin that Archie had just given him to distract him from seeing me in my undies....

I playfully offered free hugs to Archie as he delicately hip-checked me back into the bathroom.

And then he locked the door.

"You can't come out unless you have clothing on!" he instructed.

"Party-pooper!" I yelled, while my rational

mind thanked both him and the inventor of the door lock.

I changed into the bathhouse kimono-like thingy called a yukata, as Raphael told me later. My brain, the one that had a spell-induced mind of its own, realized that the only way I'd get to go to the baths was if I at least started off in the proper attire. Unfortunately, spell-brain also began calculating the so-called 'long game.'

I exited the bathroom to find that a large feast had been set out on a low table in the middle of the room.

"Come! Eat as much as you want!" Raphael announced and gestured for me to sit on a cushion next to him. And then he offered to place a piece of sashimi into my mouth.

"Why are you feeding her? She has hands," Archie grumbled, swatting at Raphael's arm.

My brain, the one that was still rational, didn't want to eat. It wanted to go hungry so the spell might turn off, as I had gleaned from the earlier conversation at the shrine.

But I happily accepted Raphael's offered food. And then I proceeded to shove food into my face until every pocket of my digestive system was full of sushi, avocado, shrimp dumplings, noodles, broth, mushrooms, tea, unidentified tempura things, mystery pickled vegetables, more shrimp dumplings, and a whole plate of colorful sweets that was delivered after Archie ate the first plate of them by himself.

Pu filled his own tummy, while simultaneously coaching Raphael on how to act cute with me, and most effectively aggravate Archie. Who, in turn, spent his time trying to make sure Raphael kept his hands to himself.

The spell-soaked side of my brain was gleeful at Archie acting jealous.

The non-spell-soaked side of my brain thought of his actions as more protective than jealous. He was acting like my older brother. Which was disappointing. More disappointing than I'd like to admit. 'How did this happen?' my rational brain asked. 'How did I acquire an older brother?'

The problem with this spell, besides the obvious one of me constantly looking like a total idiot, was that if I ever developed real feelings for Archie and tried to explain them to him, he'd never believe me.

He's just going to think it's 'Stella on the Spell' again, acting like a nutter.

Stella: The Girl Who Cried 'Hormones'

Clearly Pu hadn't thought about that part of this situation before he cast the spell. He had made it so that the truth of my heart could never be heard. Not that the truth of my heart was that I liked Archie.

No.

I mean, no.

Not really.

Well, going back to that unfeasible issue, it doesn't really matter what my feelings are. There is no feas between Archie and me. An unrealistic situation is unrealistic for a reason.

So did any of this even matter? Should I just take this flirtatious opportunity to find a realistic boyfriend for myself? I don't know. Any man who's attracted to me acting like this is probably a pervert. I quickly came to this conclusion after observing Raphael. He was a Grade A, Top of the Line Perv. He'd win the Pervert Olympics if there was such a thing. But spell-soaked Stella was also a perv and didn't seem to mind him. Exactly how long is she going to be running/ruining my life? How long could this spell last? Forever? Dear god, please, no.

After we ate more food than four beings

should ever eat in one sitting, I suggested that Archie should also change into a yukata so we could all go to the baths together. And then I wiggled my tickling fingers at him. Like a moron.

Panicked, he quickly stood up and the tiny Medusa buckler fell out of his jacket pocket. I grabbed it off the floor and hid it inside my yukata.

"If you get changed for the baths, I'll give it back to you," I said.

"I wouldn't touch that," Archie said as he reached toward the place I had hidden the shield, but stopped himself, for obvious boob-related reasons.

"You wouldn't touch what?" a woman's voice asked from behind me.

I turned around to find myself face to face with Medusa.

"Medusa from the shield?" I asked, surprised I hadn't turned to stone when I met her gaze.

"Yes, Medusa from the shield. You must be something extraordinary to call me out like this. Usually I just pull people into my world instead."

She stared at me as I watched the snakes on her

head playfully bite and hiss at each other.

"I am extraordinary! I'm the Godkiller," I answered without hesitation. "Those snakes don't ever leave your head, right?"

She smiled and winked at me.

What did that mean? Does a wink mean yes or no?

"Where's Ozzie?" she asked Archie.

"Uh. Uh, he's missing," he struggled to reply.

"Missing? Then how am I here?" she asked.

"You belong to me now," I announced. "Let's be friends!"

Would my boldness ever decrease?

"What's wrong with her head?" Medusa asked. "She's not right up there."

"It's a spell," Archie said and sighed. "Just go along with it. Can you take her to the women's baths so I can have a break?"

A break?

Ouch.

That stung.

And Medusa definitely noticed the dismal expression that appeared on my face for a split second.

"Come along, dear. It's been a long time since I've had a nice hot soak," she said as she led me out of the room.

I dwelled on the way Archie had looked overwhelmed. And yes, genuinely exhausted. Like my behavior had drained his energy completely. Yeesh. This wasn't going well for me, was it?

We walked down the hall, and turned into the women's changing room that served as an entrance to the women's baths.

"You've been here before?" I asked, noting that she knew exactly where to go.

"I used to come here occasionally with Ozzie, Archie, and Sylvie," she replied. "They've been friends with Raphael for a long time."

"You belonged to Ozzie then?"

"I did. He gave Leonardo the real Perseus Medusa shield, and in return received me."

"So Leonardo has that?"

"He does."

Suspicious old man. I'd need to be wary of him in the future.

Speaking of wary....

"Why didn't I turn into stone when I looked at you?"

"I only do that if I feel like doing it. Or if you ask me to do that to someone."

"So I guess I shouldn't tick you off, huh?"

"It's a difficult thing to do—making me angry."

Somehow she had made that into a comforting threat. Not necessarily to me. Just a vague friendly warning hanging out there in the universe. Mental note: Don't tick off Medusa.

In the changing room we disrobed and wrapped ourselves in white towels. Then she led me out to a stone-paved patio with low showers where several women were seated on stools, washing themselves before entering the very inviting, open-air, rock-lined steaming pool of hot water.

No one seemed to notice or care that one of us was a gorgon and the other one was covered in so many tattoos she looked like a human UPC symbol. I guess that wasn't noteworthy when you were inside a work of art filled with ghosts.

"So, wait. You said you usually pull people into your world. What does that mean?" I asked.

"Paintings and prints are their own worlds. Like this print we're currently in. When people want to talk with me, they usually go into my shield. Unless they're powerful enough to pull me out of it. But that's usually only in the skillset of the gods. Or Godkillers."

I still couldn't tell from her tone of voice if she

was annoyed to be called out of her shield, or just complacent with the fortunes of her life.

We finished our pre-soak showering, wrapped ourselves in our towels again, and then settled into the hot spring with deep sighs. I watched the gold light from the lanterns dance across the water's dark ripples. The night air was warm and smelled like roses. I was enjoying this, despite the high level of discomfort I was feeling from being naked around other people, complete strangers in fact. But everyone else was doing the exact same thing. So that made it easier to go along with.

That was my rational mind.

My non-rational mind was still suffering from the spell and couldn't help but think about, well, other matters.

"Do you think Archie and Raphael also went to the baths? Are there male baths here? Like this place is for women? Do you think they're there now? Do the men also get naked and wrap themselves in towels to bathe? Are there really mixed gender baths here? Do you think Archie and Raphael went there? Do you think we can go there?" I stuttered question after question to Medusa like a hyperventilating freak.

I had been holding that all in for far too long.

"You like them?" she asked, calmly. Like she was half-asleep and half-interested.

"I have to," I replied. "It's the spell. Because of it I am hopelessly infatuated with both of them."

God, at least I told her it was because of the spell.

"And they're hopelessly infatuated with you?"

"Well, clearly not. Apparently I exhaust Archie. And Raphael, he—I think he likes anything that vaguely resembles a person. It doesn't have to be me."

"I'm not sure you exhaust Archie."

"He treats me like a child."

"Are you sure? Are you not one?"

"Well."

"Archie's never seen anybody in a romantic light. They constantly throw themselves at him. So he just ignores them."

"That doesn't bode well for me, does it?"

"I'm not sure."

"Well, currently the spell just wants me to do a lot of weird stuff and see where it goes. You know. Stuff. Things."

I sounded like a moron.

Her eyebrows raised and she lazily blinked a few times while staring at me.

"It's quite an interesting spell, isn't it?" she asked.

"It's not un-crazy."

She continued to study my face while rubbing her chin thoughtfully.

"Well, I guess I can help by telling you that the men's bath is on the other side of that bamboo fence," she said, pointing to the wall in question.

Before someone could say 'steamed shrimp dumplings,' I had scrambled out of the pool up to the fence and applied myself to it. Then I started shaking it. Because that's what morons do.

All of the female ghosts yelled at me, probably with some profanities, and quickly fled the hot spring in distress at the crazy girl's actions.

Then I heard Archie's voice yell out, "Don't do that!!!"

"Do it! Do it!" Raphael and Pu chanted in unison.

Clearly they were on the other side of the fence, in the men's bath. With bare skin. Probably. And other bare stuff. Probably. Except for Pu. He'd just be furry no matter what.

Medusa joined me next to the fence and pushed it over with one touch of her fingertip, while looking in the other direction, discreetly, innocently.

As the fence slapped down into the water, Archie screamed like a child who'd just seen a mouse, crossed his arms in front of his bare chest, and sank deeper into the hot spring.

"Yessss!!!" Raphael yelled, standing up and raising his arms in triumph.

Pu was seated at the edge of the pool, wrapped in a hand towel, with his feet dangling into the hot spring. He immediately fell into a laughing fit when the fence hit the water.

"Medusa!" I commanded.

*What the heck was I going to say next?*

"Yes?"

"Turn everyone here who doesn't have romantic feelings for me into stone!"

She raised one eyebrow, and half-nodded. Then she walked over to Pu and touched him. And he turned into a stone statue of a cat, wearing underwear on his head, in a hand towel, laughing in a ball on the edge of a Japanese hot spring. Next was Raphael. Still with fists in the air and a huge grin on his face, but stone. And then she closed her eyes, touched her right eyelid, and also turned to stone.

Archie stared at her with a horrified expression.

But he wasn't stone.

And then he looked at me.

And he wasn't stone.

I stared back at him.

My mouth hung open, slightly.

And. He. Wasn't. Stone.

<u>Confession #4: The 'long game' had been much more successful than I thought it would be, thanks to my new bff, Medusa....</u>

I'm pretty sure my eyeballs started vibrating in my head at that point.

What do I do now?

What do I say now?

"You can't fall in love with me!!" we shouted, in unison, as we pointed at each other.

Unfortunately, our statements possessed drastically different intonations.

My voice = Disbelief.

His voice = A command.

What do I say now?

"Medusa, change everyone back," Archie ordered the statue. Who didn't respond. And didn't turn back into her fleshy form. "Stella, tell her to change everyone back."

"You have feelings for me," I said.

Was this still the spell talking or was it my rational brain?

No, the spell just wanted me to race toward Archie like a hormonal tornado.

The voice speaking was actually my own normal brain.

He grimaced.

The look on his face told me that he was going to try and talk his way out of this.

"Romantic feelings," I asserted. "I said 'romantic,' and here you are."

He grimaced even more.

Was he going to try and change the meaning of 'romantic' now? Was he going to say something evasive like: 'It doesn't mean anything'?

He stood up, and straightened his back, preparing to say something.

Then he sat back down in the hot spring.

Fireworks went off in my brain and all I could think about was his bare chest and the soaking wet towel clinging to the lower half of his body.

What had we been talking about?

What was my name?

Where were we?

"You do do something to my heart," he practically whispered.

Did he just say doo-doo?

No, wait.

The vibrating eyeballs and brain fireworks combined into a persistent hum in my head. Or was I actually just humming? *Was I really just standing here humming?!?* What song is this?! The Battle Hymn of the Republic?!? God, stop it. It's not possible for you to be more of a freak!

But did he just say what I think he said?

I do something to his heart?

Like angina? Or something else?

How should a person act in this scenario? Cool? Demure? Shy? This kind of situation had never presented itself to me before.

"But I can't be with you," he continued.

"*Why not?!*" I blurted. "You saved me from Lontano! According to feudal law you have to marry me and take responsibility for me now that you've saved my life! It's your obligation!"

He looked up from the water ripples that he'd been staring at and met my gaze.

What in the *bloody heck* was I even saying?!?!

*Feudal law?!?!*

I didn't even know what feudal law was.

Marry me? Take responsibility for me?!? Obligation?!

What year was this? 1492?

I was making myself cringe so much I think my skin might start retreating inside my own body like a human sundried tomato. How was this man ever going to take me seriously?

"Are your feelings not profound enough?!" I pushed.

"Perhaps we could be together if this was a different situation."

A different situation?

Like one where I wasn't under a spell?

Or one where I wasn't a sixteen-year-old girl?

"I'll be eighteen in just over a year!" I cried out.

Yes, Stella. Like *that* matters. In the grand scheme of schemes, your age is the one thing keeping you two apart. Yes, that's it. That's the only thing. You moron.

"I," Archie began.

No. No. I didn't want to hear what came next.

He's romantically interested in me *but....*

It was that 'but.'

I didn't want to hear the but.

I didn't need to hear a list of all of my faults and

inadequacies.

I didn't need him to say out loud why I wasn't good enough for him.

I wanted to clamp my hands over my ears.

But the spell was still in effect and it was pulsing in my head: 'flirt with him, flirt with him.' *Didn't it see a lost cause when one presented itself?!?!*

"I," Archie repeated.

Okay, if I pick up one of these rocks and hurl it at him, maybe he'll stop talking.

Right?

But he didn't say anything.

Well, not right away.

He looked around the hot spring, at the stone statues, and then at me.

Then he smiled. At me. Like the most genuine, warm smile I'd ever seen.

His whole face lit up and I knew at once that all was right in the world. Butterflies were happily flapping their wings. Puppies were wagging their tails. Flowers were blooming their blooms. And my heart melted into a buttery goop in my chest. I think my throat started to make a gurgling sound all on its own. That smile was all I ever needed in my life.

"What did you just ask me?" he asked.

What the *what*?

Was I not the only one here losing their mind to metabolic chemicals?

"Are your feelings not profound enough?" I asked again in a knee-jerk reaction.

I guess that was what I was most curious about. Mystery solved in that department. Stupid mouth. Stupid brain.

"My feelings?" he asked.

"Your romantic feelings for me. You have some, obviously, or else you'd be a stone sculpture, too. So are they not profound enough for you to be with me?"

His eyes shifted from side to side for an instant, and then it looked like a tiny light went on inside his brain.

"Ahh, I see," he said, standing up.

He stepped up out of the pool and began to walk toward me.

If I wasn't spell-Stella, I would turn around, jump back into the women's bath, scramble my way across it, and run out into the bathhouse to find a box to hide myself in.

But the spell was still in effect, so I just stood my ground, hands on my hips, staring him down.

I guess in what I assumed was a flirty way.

He walked closer and closer, keeping his eyes glued to mine. His skin glistened in the moonlight. His black hair was slicked back, little drops of water falling from it with each step forward.

I needed to fake a stomach ache. I needed to do that right now. But I couldn't. I didn't. Could I step on my own foot and break a toe? Bludgeon myself with one of these rocks? Trip myself, fall into the hot spring and drown? But my body didn't move to do any of those things. Instead it shifted its alignment toward the incoming Archie.

God, no, no. Stop. What's happening? What's about to happen here???

He was about five feet away from me when he seemed to change his mind about something. A little grin passed across his face as he looked down at the ground.

"You're so beautiful," he said as he looked back up at me.

Did I just start crying?

I think I just started crying.

God, Stella. Do you have to make your emotional frailty so obvious?!? Why don't you just tattoo the word 'desperate' across your darn forehead?!?

"You must, you must," I stuttered, with remarkable finesse.

*What was I even trying to say?!*

"I'm glad that we're alone," he said, as he glanced at the statues. "Sort of."

My heart had definitely started beating faster than a normal human heart should beat.

"I only ever wanted to be alone with you," he continued, smiling coyly at the ground.

What in the heck was happening?

"And to have you as my partner would only be fitting," he said.

*What in the heck was happening?!*

"What do you think?" he asked. "Do you want to be with me, forever?"

The little hairs on the back of my neck stood on end.

"What do you say? Do you want to be with this stupid boy forever?" he pushed.

I took a step backward.

"This stupid Archie," he said, as he took a step toward me.

I took another step backward.

His gaze was piercing. His dancing eyes had

stopped their waltzing and were now just pene-trating my soul.

"Do you know who I am?" he asked, sternly.

*Ssssshhhhhhpppptt.*

"*Mia bella ragazza,*" he whispered, stepping even closer to me.

He grinned at me with an intense mischiev-ousness.

"Still super creepy," I said, fiercely staring back at him. "Lontano."

"Did you miss me?" he asked.

Then he took another step toward me, still smiling broadly.

That was Archie's smile that Lontano was stealing. And giving to me.

It was the kind of transformative smile that spread across his face like a match igniting, mak-ing him glow with happiness. It was perfection. It made suns shine. Planets rotate. Hearts beat. It made lifetimes worth living. Dances worth dan-cing. Songs worth singing. Hugs worth giving.

It completely changed Archie's air of unattain-able nobility.

And it was a gift that I had so desperately wanted, without even realizing it.

So I was quite ticked off that it wasn't actually

Archie smiling at me like I was the most beautiful person in the world. Like I was the most important thing in his life. Like he loved and accepted me just as I was, and would do so forever. Striding toward me, half-naked, dripping wet, and smiling that golden, glorious smile.

No, no. This wasn't good.

I could feel the spell wanting to reach out for him.

But it's not really Archie, spell! It's not really Archie!!!

"*Gossshhdarnnit!!! Belly-fun!!!*" I shouted at my bracelet, shaking my wrist.

And out popped my dashing warrior on a Pegasus, armed with a long pointy stick.

"What now?" he asked as he jumped off his flying pony and landed with a thud next to me, slightly cracking the stone walkway.

Archie, or rather, Lontano looked surprised. Thank god. At least I had managed to match his unexpected entrance with one of my own. Although I wasn't sure how the rest of this was going to go.

"Somebody else is in Archie's mind. Can you get him out of there?" I asked, pointing toward Archie's head, angrily. "He's not in there with permission."

And with that request, Bellerophon gracefully swung his stick through the air and cracked Archie over the side of the head with it, sending the poor god sailing face-first into the women's hot spring.

"He'll be fine now," Bellerophon said. "Just make sure he doesn't drown in there. Gods hate drowning."

And then the bracelet zapped the warrior man and his flying horse back to their world, just as quickly as they had shown up.

I clambered down into the pool where Archie was now floating, facedown, completely out. I struggled to turn and lift his body so that his breathing-face-holes were above water. Then I scooted my way across the pool and leaned against the side, holding Archie against my body so he wouldn't sink back down into the water.

Was this Archie I was holding? Or Lontano?

Was direct concussion-inducing violence all that was necessary to knock Lontano out of Archie's mind? Had that worked? Would it have worked if I'd done it? Or would it only work with Belly-fun doing it with his stick?

"Medusa, change back. And change the others

back, too!" I shouted, hoping my words would carry if I screeched them loud enough.

Soon a dignified Medusa, a talking cat with underwear on its head, and an amorous Italian ghost joined me. All in their fleshy forms. All soaking wet. And all wondering what the heck I was doing.

"My game of flirtation didn't end up going as I wanted it to," I announced.

"Did you beat him to death?" Pu asked. "Because he wouldn't submit to your cutesy ways?"

"No. Can someone help me get him out of the water?" I pleaded.

# CHAPTER FIFTEEN.

*What Happens in Switzerland Stays in Switzerland.*

*By Morrow.*

(Maple: Switzerland doesn't really roll off the tongue like Vegas, does it?)

"*Aaagggghhhhh!!!!!*" Lontano screamed as he woke up and grabbed his head.

He seemed to be in great pain, and his nose started bleeding the instant he sat up in bed. I was on watch, so I witnessed the whole thing. But it's not like I knew what was going on just because I had seen it happen.

Everyone else woke up at his caterwauling, and Hercules suggested, groggily, that he could do Lontano the favor of knocking him unconscious so we could all go back to sleep.

But Lontano just groaned in response, curled up in a ball, and held his legs against his body.

I went into the bathroom and got a towel for his nosebleed. He took it without saying anything, and held it against his face.

Sometimes he reminded me of a tiny, abandoned kitten that you just wanted to scoop up, plop inside your jacket, and take home. I needed to keep telling myself that this kitten was actually a dangerous, unpredictable nutjob.

"Do you want me to hold you in my arms?" Ellie offered, reaching out, and smiling like a loon. "For comfort."

Apparently she was thinking the same way I was. Although the perverted glint in her eyes suggested that she had slightly different thoughts on the matter than I did. Luckily, she was on the other bed and far enough away from him that I wasn't too worried that she'd actually try to hold him. And luckily, Lontano just looked at her like he was concerned for her mental wellbeing.

"Suit yourself," she said. "I'll just hug myself over here. Forever alone."

My sisters and I stared at Lontano. We were

all wide awake, slightly panicked, and pretending not to be. Hercules had already fallen back asleep, clearly not concerned at all.

Silence crept back into the room as we waited for something to happen. Was he going to go back to sleep? Was he going to jump up and try to disembowel us? What was he going to do? Sit there and bleed out?

He mostly just looked like he wanted to cry.

"That backfired," he whispered, after several minutes had passed.

Who was he saying that to?

To Ellie? To me? To himself?

"What backfired?" Nora asked, clearly misreading his somber mumbling as an invitation to conversation.

"Nothing," Lontano replied. "Nothing at all."

"Did we do that to him?" I asked my sisters.

"Wasn't me," Nora responded.

"I don't think so," Ellie added.

"I did it to myself," he said, and then sighed. "Next time I'll have to be more subtle."

"Next time you do what?" I asked.

"The next time I stare into the meaningless abyss of life."

What was that supposed to mean?

My sisters and I exchanged a confused look.

Had he tried to cast a spell on us and it had gone back onto him because of our spell? I hadn't felt that happen. Whatever he'd done, it didn't seem like it was connected to us.

So what had it been?

"Was it a nightmare?" Nora asked. "I once had a nightmare that the creepy monkey's paw from that old story was resting against my face as I slept, occasionally wiggling its fingers."

Lontano's brow furrowed as he glanced over at Nora, a look of bewilderment enveloping his face.

"But then I woke up and it was only Morrow's hand on my face because she had crawled into my bed during a thunderstorm," Nora finished.

"I'm glad you can always find such relevant discussion topics to share with us, Norad," Ellie said. Then she sighed and rolled her eyes.

"So you three are sisters, right?" Lontano asked.

"Yes," Nora responded, clearly without thinking.

"Interesting," he replied, and then checked the towel to see if his nosebleed had stopped. It hadn't.

"Does that matter?" Ellie asked.

"Well, I have noticed one thing about you three," he replied.

"What's that?" I asked, curious, but also a little freaked out that he was studying us.

"A slight similarity in your smell to two people I once met."

"Our smell? What are you? A scent hound?" I asked.

"I do have a more gifted nose than most people," he said, and then smirked. "As a Demi-God of Death one must have a heightened sense of smell to identify those who are about to die, those who I have to take with me into the Realm of the Dead."

"So you smell dead people?" Nora asked.

"Um. Sort of. More like, about-to-be-dead people. But back to my main point—those two people I once met."

"What about 'em?" I asked, trying to imbue my words with bored disinterest.

"If you're nice to me, perhaps I will introduce you to those two people. It was a man and a woman. Perhaps a husband and his wife? I feel like I should've known their names. But I just never marked them down in my brain."

He tapped the side of his head nonchalantly, but he was looking at each of us, in turn. Trying to gauge our reaction to this information.

Honestly, I didn't know how to react. Because I had no idea what the heck he was talking about. But Ellie's back straightened. And Nora sucked her teeth. Did that mean they knew what he was talking about?

"Oh, I'll *always* be nice to you," Ellie answered sweetly. "But if you only met them once, how do you know where they are to introduce us to them?"

"I currently have them in my possession. Or should I say, I have them in storage," he said, and then smiled.

"So are they dead or alive?" I asked.

"That could go either way. I guess you could say that they're alive. But they could also be killed at any moment. Sort of like those two lejerdemani with the rabbit."

And his intent staring continued. He really wanted to see us flinch. He wanted a reaction. He wanted us to say something and give away who we really were.

"I like rabbits," Nora said. "They make me think of pigs. And tea. I once drank a mug of tea so fast that I burned my throat. I had forgotten it was hot. I thought I was going to die. I couldn't stomach hot tea for a long time after that."

Lontano's brow furrowed again.

Nora had clearly caught on to what he was doing, and was using her incessant insanity to prevent any logic from entering the conversation. Good ol' Freakish Norad the Weirdo.

"Speaking of drinking things, we should have an eating battle at breakfast. Whoever eats the most, wins," she continued. "How long until they serve breakfast? What time is it now?"

"The sun isn't even up yet," I said.

Then she proceeded to babble on about what dishes she hoped would be served at breakfast, and somehow the conversation (with herself) got to the point where she was describing a tree that she had once seen foaming at the mouth like it had rabies.

Lontano fell back asleep or pretended to, still curled up against his bed's headboard.

Meanwhile, I wondered what had just happened.

A man and a woman who smelled like us? A married couple perhaps? What did that mean? And what did that have to do with us being sisters? Ahhh. Ohhh. Duh. He was wondering if that man and woman in his possession were our parents. Were they? Could they be? I thought they were dead.

I looked over at Ellie with epiphany and hopeful expectation in my eyes. She just looked back solemnly, and slowly shook her head in a bored manner as if to say, 'Don't say a word, you halfwit. Don't give anything away.'

She was right. Lontano was not the kind of person you would want to know your secrets. And he already knew too much. He even knew how we smelled. So we'd have to be even more careful with our words in the future.

A couple hours later, Holbein burst into our room and declared, "I will give you my most famous lost work of art!"

Hercules immediately rolled off the couch he'd been sleeping on—or rather—he'd been crushing into a couch pancake. He looked at Holbein and seemed to be deciding whether or not to smack him for waking him up.

"Can it be a sculpture? A beautiful woman, with good-looking—bone structure?" Hercules asked, choosing his words carefully after briefly looking at me.

"In what universe was I a sculptor?" Holbein asked. "Not this one. Sure, I designed a few things here and there. Fountains. Jewelry. So on. But I never made anything like you."

"Darnit," Hercules replied and then sat back down on the couch, which really couldn't be called a couch anymore.

"We were amazingly triumphant in our win last evening," Holbein continued. "So I will gift you the Whitehall Mural. Unfortunately it does include Henry VIII in it, but it's still a very important work, so we'll just pretend that pretentious butthole is not in it. Toodles!!!"

He tossed a tiny box to Nora, who caught it with one hand. Then he waved and left the room.

And we were back at the game board, all sitting on the ground.

George the Goose was seated at a table several yards away eating lunch.

"Thank god there's food!" Nora said as she scrambled onto her feet, sat herself at George's table, and began to devour two sandwiches at once, one in each hand.

Ellie and I joined her, with Lontano trailing behind.

Nora had set the tiny box down on the table without thinking, and Lontano grabbed it, opened it, and tapped twice on whatever was inside.

And then he disappeared, and the box dropped onto the ground.

"*Whaaaaattttttt?!?!?!*" Nora yelled, standing up, dropping sandwich bits out of her mouth.

"What the! He's not supposed to be able to go anywhere that isn't next to me!" Ellie cried out, almost whining, while pointing at the box.

"Don't worry, he'll be back in a minute," George said, calmly. "He thinks he's escaping, but he can't do that when Archie's still in the game. Those two are like peanut butter and jelly pressed between two slices of bread right now. Gosh, I'm hungry. I forgot to eat breakfast."

George tapped on the table with his wing and more food appeared. Then he whistled (can a goose really whistle???) and a large block of marble appeared next to the table so that Hercules had a non-crushable place to sit.

And then we waited.

Well, we ate. And waited.

"Where exactly did he go?" I asked, after having sucked down two bowls of tomato soup garnished by piles of deliciously salty cheddar crackers.

"Inside the Whitehall Mural," George said. "There's a tiny cube in that box that serves as a key to the mural, which was destroyed by a fire in 1698. So it exists as part of the Whitehall Palace in the Realm of Destruction. You must have met Holbein. He owns the key to the mural, so he can go in and out of it anytime whether he's in the Realm or not."

"So Lontano will try to go into the mural, and then come out of it into the Realm of Destruction, outside of the game?" Hercules asked.

"He'll try," George said. "At least I assume so."

Our happy brunch continued, all of us more concerned about our growling stomachs than what in the world Lontano was doing right now.

He did eventually reappear.

Swearing.

And then he proceeded to try and stomp the tiny box to smithereens. But it was impervious to his angry foot and didn't acquire a scratch.

Then he joined us at the table, began eating, and pretended like nothing had just happened.

"That Henry VIII is such a turdhole, no matter which version of him you meet," he muttered in between mouthfuls of a toasted ham and cheese sandwich. "Mmmm. Capocollo di Calabria. And Parrano. Mmmmm. Are these kalamata olives in this bread? God, this is good."

"See? You should just enjoy the moment, instead of trying to fight against the tide," George said.

Lontano sighed, kept chewing fervently, and said nothing.

"I could spend all day watching you eat," Ellie said. "I'd pay to watch a movie of you eating. Just eating."

"Stop that," he said as he blinked heavily at her.

She responded by making a kissy face at him.

"Also, I'm well aware that I told you all last night that I turned Riot as Verbena into a plant, but that doesn't mean I'm going to tell you all of my secrets like a ninny," he said.

"Ninny-ninny-poo-poo," Nora responded, with a smile.

"There was absolutely no need to cast that 'loose lips' thing onto me whatsoever," he said, as he glared at her.

"I don't know. It seemed like you had a lot to get off your chest, almost as if you *wanted* us to know," Ellie replied.

"Not true. Not true. I told you that she's a plant and that she's in India, but I didn't tell you where in India. There's a difference between a spell-induced slip of the tongue and purposeful explication."

"Really? Are you sure? Because you didn't even tell us she was in India last night and today you just did. Are you sure you aren't doing this on purpose?" Ellie asked.

A look of disappointed annoyance sunk into Lontano's face.

"Well, I didn't tell you *which* India, right?" he asked.

"I'm not sure it's possible for you to be more confusing," I said.

"Good," he replied.

Two seconds later, we were sitting on the floor in front of an ornate doorway with an eerie winged skeleton hanging over it—sandwiches still in hand, crackers still in mouths, soup still being swallowed.

# CHAPTER SIXTEEN.

*What Happens at a Japanese Bathhouse Stays at a Japanese Bathhouse.*

*By Stella.*

(Stella: Why isn't there some asinine middle name up there for me this time? Have you run out of stupid ideas for that?

Maple: Sssssshhhh. I'm trying to concentrate here. Stop distracting me with your foolish requests for foolish middle names. I'm trying to write a book here. Yeesh.

Stella: *So now I'm interrupting you?!?!*

Maple: Yes! You rude butthole.

Stella: I...can't even. Sigh.)

After we were dry, dressed, and reestablished in Raphael's rooms, I explained what had happened at the hot spring as Archie laid on the floor with a cool, wet washcloth on his bruised head. He still hadn't woken up.

"That #$%&@ Lontano," Pu said, along with several other un-publish-able, and un-spell-able curse words. "*Just what does he think he's doing?!*"

"Do you think he's still in there?" I asked.

"We'll only know when he wakes up. If he wakes up," Pu replied. "Bellerophon is capable of killing a god, for the Godkiller."

A look of total horror engulfed my face.

Oh, god.

Had I killed him?!

"He'll wake up. He's fine. I know what dead looks like, and that's not it," Raphael added, gently poking Archie in the ribs.

"So Tiziano is now Lontano? And he shares some of Archie's powers?" Medusa asked.

"Yes. Sort of," Pu said.

"That's unfortunate. He was always a very persistent fellow," Medusa said.

"Sadly, he's also a nutjob now," Pu said. "A persistent nutjob."

"It sounds to me like he wants to control Stella, even from within Archie, if that's how he can accomplish it," Medusa added.

Control me? I guess that's what it was. And if there's one thing a teenage girl doesn't like, it's someone trying to control her. He's a penguin's fishy butthole, that jerk.

Becoming Archie? The most attractive man I had ever set eyes on? He was trying to manipulate me. And if there's a second thing a teenage girl doesn't like, it's someone trying to manipulate her.

(Honestly, teenage girls really hate a lot of things, but we'll stick with those two for now.)

"I wanted to help him fix his sister," I said. "I felt like I should at least try. But now I just want to punch him. Archie got the crap smacked out of his head because of that jerk. Did he really think this was going to get me to help him? His logic is flawed."

"That's not the only thing that's flawed about him," Raphael commented.

Archie's eyes fluttered open, and he sat up, only to grab his head in his hands and groan.

"Dear god," he said. "What the heck just happened?"

"What was the first thing I fed Stella at dinner?" Raphael asked him.

"Ahi sashimi. Even though I told you repeatedly not to touch her," Archie responded, glaring at him.

"That's not Lontano," Raphael confirmed.

"What's not Lontano?" Archie asked.

So the story was told a second time.

Only this time, I was completely mortified that Archie was hearing about the whole conversation concerning his possibly profound romantic feelings for me while I was sitting right next to him, turning beet-red.

"Do you remember when he actually took over your mind? Could you sense it happening?" Pu asked.

Oh, yes. God. Tell me. What were your words and what were his words?

I mean, no. I mean, yes. Wait.

Had the whole thing just been Lontano?

Were those romantic feelings really his?

Don't tell me! Don't tell me anything!

"I remember her saying she would be eighteen in just over a year," he replied.

"Ooohhh, good girl, good girl," Pu said, slapping me on the back. "Did you tell her you'd wait for her, as you held her hand?"

"No," Archie said. "I don't remember what I did after that. But I didn't say she was beautiful.

That wasn't me."

Accckkkk.

Thank you.

No need to spare my feelings or anything.

"So she's not beautiful?" Raphael asked, winking at Archie. "I think she is."

He blew me a kiss.

"She's not beautiful," Archie replied, looking like he was about to smack Raphael.

This. This was not going well for me.

"She's more than beautiful," Archie continued.

He glared at Raphael but then shyly looked down at his hands.

"Ooohhh, good save, good save," Pu said.

"How about—how about if you say 'you're beautiful' to me then I'll know it's Lontano. Because he tells me that all the time. And you can barely look me in the eye," I said to Archie. "I need some way to tell it's not you. So if I ask you, 'Am I beautiful?' And you say, 'Yes.' Then I'll know it's not you."

There. I saved myself in more than one way. Yeesh.

'She's more than beautiful.' My butt. Who was he kidding? That was the least convincing thing I've heard all year. People living on Mars in the future could see that he was just trying to spare my feelings after he said I wasn't beautiful.

"Alright," Archie agreed. "I won't say you're beautiful."

My heart splintered a little. Why was it reading meaning into something that meant nothing? Goshdarn heart.

"So you couldn't tell he was invading your mind?" Medusa asked, more concerned about the real issue at hand.

"No. One moment I was thinking about Stella being eighteen and the next minute I woke up here, with a horrible headache."

"I wonder what you'll look like when you're eighteen," Raphael said and then grinned at me.

"She'll probably still look like a child," Pu said. "That's what she looks like now—a child. Well, a sickly one. Pale, skinny, flat chested. With a tired, worn-out face. And sad, glazed-over, droopy eyes."

Speaking of people who were penguin's fishy buttholes...

"I'll put a spell in place that'll help block him from entering my mind. But you all need to be prepared in case this happens again. He and I are still bonded by the power transfer spell he cast.

So keep an eye on me at all times," Archie said. "It's a good thing you thought of Bellerophon, Stella. Use him whenever you need to, whenever I start acting weird."

So your skull can get cracked open again?

Had he thought that statement through before he said it?

"You know what's the most disappointing aspect of all this?" Pu asked.

"What?" I inquired.

"The whole scenario of you flirting with Archie and him revealing his feelings for you was completely ruined," Pu whined.

And then Archie had a coughing fit.

I'm pretty sure it was acting.

But really? That was what Pu was most concerned about? Hadn't he understood that Lontano was now a bigger, more pressing danger to all of us?

Plus, how was I supposed to successfully flirt with a man who I couldn't even be sure was himself at any given moment?

Wait, why was I doing that?

Oh, right. To see Archie smile again. At me.

Because my mind is just that hopelessly simple.

What a moron.

"Has Lontano ever tried to kiss you?" Pu asked as we began to settle down for the evening, i.e. set up our roll-out mattresses in respective 'boy' and 'girl' areas of Raphael's rooms.

Both Archie and Raphael froze in the midst of unfolding blankets to listen.

"No, not really. Although I don't think it's out of the question. He acts like a—I don't know —a really creepy, handsome dude. Sort of perverted, but in a menacing way," I explained. "In my dream, he almost kissed me, I think. But then I woke up."

Archie's grip on his pink, embroidered blankie tightened, his knuckles turning white.

"Hmmm. Too bad. I was going to tell Archie that he should kiss you as a sign that it's him and not Lontano," Pu said, smirking.

"Ha. Ha. Good one. Not," I replied. "Wait, why are you asking if Lontano has ever tried to kiss me? You've either been in my head or next to me this whole time. So you know everything I know."

"I know. And that's *sooo* depressing, on *sooo* many levels. But I figured I should bring up the topic, out loud, just the same. Just in case

I missed something, somewhere," Pu answered, and then grinned at Archie.

Archie grumbled something under his breath, and went back to his blanket arrangements.

"Have you ever kissed *anyone*?" Raphael asked me, his face glowing with curiosity.

Archie's blanket arrangements halted once again.

My mind went blank.

Had I kissed someone?

Had that happened?

My life had been such a blur lately that I couldn't quite know for sure.

"I don't know," I said as I glanced over at Archie.

He was technically the only one I'd ever been 'alone' with, given the Pu situation. But I don't think I was ever alone with him and under the spell simultaneously.

Or was I?

"She's done weird things to Archie's hands, fingers, chest, ears, and hair—but she's never kissed his lips," Pu said as he ticked off the list on his tiny, pink paw pads.

Oh, god. Why'd he have to do that? Shut up, furball.

"Well, Archie's kissed a lot of girls. I mean—*A LOT*," Raphael said.

Archie looked at Raphael like he wanted his head to split open.

"They kiss me. Women, and some men, they just kiss me. Sometimes. It just happens," Archie said, looking like he was desperately trying to send these excuses to my ears.

"Oh. Yes. That makes it better. And all okay. Somehow," Raphael added, winking at Archie.

How many women had kissed him?

I wasn't really worried about the men.

I mean, I might have to visualize that later to really comprehend it.

But how many women had thrown their lips onto his? Was it truly possible for someone to be the center of so much affection and yet not be interested in anyone? That didn't seem normal.

But he had said that I do something to his heart.

Or doo-doo something to his heart.

Perhaps we really are fated to fall in love?

No, no, no. No.

That's just silly.

Medusa, who'd been observing this whole conversation like a psychologist during a group therapy session, clicked her tongue at me, and motioned that I should join her in the bathroom.

"I think I need to help you again," she said once the door was closed.

"Ooo, ooo. Good. Help me come up with a strategy for how I can flirt with Archie tonight," I replied. "A scenario where he doesn't lock me in the bathroom."

"Um, no. That's not where I was going with this."

"I definitely need your help though. I'm so nervous around him and I'm not even in a relationship with him. What's wrong with me? Every time he does something, even putting a pastry in his mouth, I grin like a weirdo. Sometimes he's so cute I feel the need to slap myself."

"I also feel the need to slap someone," Medusa said and sighed. "How do we get rid of this spell?"

"I don't know."

"Okay, well can I at least talk to you about Lontano without you losing your mind? I think you need a more foolproof way to tell that it's Lontano in Archie's head than you saying 'Am I beautiful?' and he says 'Yeah.' I mean, who's writing this crap? That's just lame and probably won't work at all."

"You'd have to ask Maple about that. I just say my lines and try not to think too much. If I question her logic she never really responds in a helpful manner."

"Alright, alright. Let's call up Secretezza. She's an old friend of mine. She'll help us."

"You have a secretary?"

Medusa's obligatory eye-roll was followed by specific instructions for how I could call up the Icon of Secrecy.

A gorgeous, but very stern-looking, woman with an arty goth fashion sense zapped out of my bracelet and joined us in the bathroom.

"Why do people always call me up when they're in the john?" she asked. "Medusa, what's up? How ya been?"

They exchanged pleasantries while my mind drifted back to Archie and imagined ways I could offer him a shoulder massage later.

"Tezza, she needs to borrow your ring for a while," Medusa said to the woman, while pointing at me.

"The Jainkohiltzaile?" the woman asked, looking at me quizzically. "For her, then, yes."

She slipped off one of her rings, the one which

featured a slightly protruding keyhole shape in the center of it, and handed it to me.

"When you want to know someone's secrets, you push this ring into their flesh, and all will be revealed," Medusa explained.

"You don't need to push that hard," Tezza said. "No need to punch it through someone's head or anything. I mean, you can punch them if they deserve it. But otherwise, you can just touch it to their chest enough to make full contact."

"Not just their chest though," Medusa added. "Archie's chest is barely ever bare. And after the baths, well, the chances are even slimmer. Any bare skin will work. Use it to figure out if, or when, Lontano is in Archie's head."

Ahhhhhh. I get it now.

Also—a ring that will make anybody tell me their secrets??? *Wth?!?!* Where had this marvel of magical engineering been all of my life?!?!

Wait, who would I have used this on?

I don't have any friends.

Okay, I'd at least have used it on my father. Wow, that's really sad and pathetic.

Although, my father is the person with the most secrets that I probably want to know.

But then again, there's Archie. Is that what falling in love is? You suddenly want to know more about your crush's secrets than your father's secrets? Well, either way, it's still really sad and pathetic.

"Also, I need another favor," Medusa said to Tezza. "Raphael is here and you need to distract him because he's harassing Archie by fake-flirting with this girl, and I just can't watch it anymore."

"One: You could just go back into your shield and spare your own eyes and ears," Tezza replied.

"But then this girl would be on her own," Medusa answered. "And she's got enough problems already."

"Two: You should've started this conversation with 'Raphael is here.' That's definitely one person I need to work some stuff out with. I'd be delighted to 'distract' him."

Tezza whipped the bathroom door open and strode out into the main room to stare Raphael down. Upon seeing her, his face became a textbook illustration of 'sheer panic.'

"Raph! So I've been talking with Forte about that time we were all in Greece together," Tezza said. "And I think there's some things you never told me about."

"Archie, word of advice, don't ever start anything with any of the icons!" he said as he slapped him on the shoulder, and then unceremoniously fled the room.

"We haven't even talked about a task for the game yet!" Archie called out.

But he was already gone, with Tezza on his heels.

"Don't worry. He'll be back eventually," Medusa said. "For now, I'm going back to my place. You wanna come with me, furball? I just made a batch of cinnamon rolls before I was zapped here."

Pu, the furball in question, gladly accompanied Medusa back into her shield, with only a wink and a comment that he'd be back in the morning.

Archie and I.

Archie and I.

Archie, the ring of revealed secrets, and I.

"It appears as if every time we spend a night together in this story, it'll just be the two of us," he remarked, as he dragged his mattress to the far corner of the room, and sat down on it with his back against the wall.

He didn't have to make it so obvious he was

avoiding me.

'Do something cute so he starts talking with you,' spell-brain said.

'Put the ring on him,' semi-rational brain said.

I needed a third, normal brain for moments like this.

I slipped the ring onto the middle finger of my right hand and turned the keyhole shape to be on the same side as my palm. I *really* wanted to apply this to Archie and ask him why we couldn't be together. Was that a possibility? Should I even do that? That seemed wrong.

I stared at the ring for a while.

And then I looked at Archie.

He was now pretending to be asleep, but I could tell his eyes weren't completely closed. He was watching me as much as I was watching him.

I sat down on my mattress.

Do something cute. Do something cute. Do something cute.

I snapped my fingers and somehow cast a giant jar of puffed cheese balls into existence.

"How'd you do that?!" Archie gasped, clearly not asleep.

"I don't know!" I also gasped. "I just thought

about it and it happened!"

"Oh."

He shifted his weight and 'closed' his eyes again.

Making cheese balls doesn't count as cute, Stella.

I opened the jar and began lobbing the orange orbs at him while making 'brrrring, brrrring' noises like a ringing telephone. This must be spell-brain. No sane person would do this. I don't think this counts as cute, spell-brain.

He sighed. Deeply. And dodged a ball by leaning out of its range. Totally not asleep.

I scooted across the floor a bit, trying to get closer so my puffed projectiles could reach him more easily. He scooted to the left as a handful of them landed on his mattress where he should've been. How was he so fast?

I tried again, but he kept sliding out of the way like melting butter on a frying pan.

One eye opened. So I threw a cheese ball at it. Which he dodged.

"Whatcha doin'?" he asked as he stood up.

Oh, so he's gonna be a moving target, huh?

I tossed more cheese balls at him as an answer.

He stepped out of their way. So I threw more.

And more. Until there was a whole amazing ballet of one tuxedo'd man dancing away from puffed cheese.

I started giggling.

He started giggling.

And then he started grabbing handfuls of cheese balls and whizzing them at me as he circled the room.

I was laughing so hard I was starting to wheeze unattractively.

I took a break from throwing puffs to catch my breath, and in a flash he knelt down on the floor next to me and grabbed my cheese-ball-throwing hand. Which happened to be my right hand. My ring hand.

"Okay, you can stop now," he said in between giggles. "The whole room is covered in these things. How about we go to sleep before this gets even more silly?"

But he didn't let go of my hand.

He was just holding it.

Wait.

What?

Nooooo. Wait. Yeeeesssss.

But the ring! Use the ring, you moron!

"Why can't we be together?!" I squeaked.

"Uh, I—I killed your mother," he replied.

"*What?!*"

Was this the ring of revealed craziness instead of the ring of revealed secrets?

"I mean, my inaction killed your mother. And a bunch of other people. A whole lot of people died because I wasn't paying attention," he said. "And now I have to fix it, but I haven't yet. So everything is still messed up, and everyone is gone."

"Oh."

That's *a lot* of reasons.

"And now I'm alone," he said. "And I don't know how this will end."

"But you're not alone. I'm right here."

"And you may be enough."

He squeezed my hand, and I squeezed back.

"*Wait, god, what is this?!*" he asked as he let go of my hand and looked at the faint keyhole-shaped impression on his palm. "*What is this???*"

Then he grabbed my hand again and examined Tezza's ring. I would describe his expression as the '*what have you done?!*' look. I smiled at him. God knows why. I guess I was trying to downplay my own evilness.

"Are you Lontano in Archie's head?" I asked, retreating to the real reason I had the ring, trying to save my own butt. "I'm using Secretezza's ring to find out."

"No, I'm Archie in Archie's head."

"Are you happy that it's just us right now?"

"Yes."

His face turned bright red, with a look of terrified constipation. Surprised at his own reply, he dropped my hand like a hot potato, and rubbed the back of his neck while staring at the floor.

"What exactly does this ring do?" he asked.

"It's sort of like a 'I cannot tell a lie' ring, I think."

I didn't want to say it revealed secrets. Then it sounded sinister. Cough.

"Have you ever dated a Godkiller before?" I may have asked....

"No. I've never dated anyone before. Ugh, no. Wait," he said as he tried to scour the keyhole-shape out of his palm with his thumb.

"Do gods date? Is that a thing?"

"Yeah, sort of."

"But you've never dated anyone?"

"No. It would cause too many problems. Are you really going to keep asking me questions like this? I've already proven I'm me and not

Lontano."

"I have to be thorough. If you could see one person right now, any person, who would it be?"

"Ozzie."

"Ozzie? He's your friend?"

"My best friend. Was my best friend. Is my best friend. I don't know if he's still alive."

"Oh."

"I mean, I think he's still alive. But maybe not. If not, I'm the only one left."

"Oh. Could I be your friend?"

"Of course."

"Could I be a more-than-friends friend?"

"Aacckkkgggghhhhhhhh," he gasped as he stood up, scrambled over to his mattress, and shoved his face into his pink blanket to force himself to stop talking.

"Do you wanna hold hands more?" I asked.

"Yaaaaarrgghhhhh."

I couldn't help but giggle. God, this was adorable. He was still dangerously attractive, don't get me wrong. But this was a new type of endearing charm.

That's it.

I'm never giving this ring back.

# CHAPTER SEVENTEEN.

*The Beginning of Death.*

*By Morrow.*

We were in a white, empty room except for the doorway and the skeleton, which looked like a three-dimensional red chalk sketch.

The skeleton was half-hidden by drapery, so it was difficult to get a clear look at it. But there was definitely a huge hourglass in its right hand. The sand inside slid gently down into the bottom chamber. Soon the top portion was empty. Obviously, it had been upended right before our arrival.

Then what I had regarded as eerie turned into downright frightening.

The skeleton shifted its weight against the top

of the doorway, pushed off its shroud, stretched its wings out, and yawned.

I thought it was about to fly down from the top of the doorway, but the doors opened and a janitor wheeled a mop and bucket into the room. He started swishing away at the floor while listening to 80s Pop on his headphones, not even acknowledging us.

"Well, someone has to keep this place clean," the winged skeleton said to us.

The janitor then tipped his hat at him, but ignored us completely.

"Congratulations. You're dead," the skeleton continued. "You've arrived at the Death space on the Game of Goose board. Your body has been entombed in a Friedrich cemetery painting. Don't worry, you won't start decaying or anything. This is a game after all. But you are dead, and technically you're now a ghost."

Then he flitted down from the doorway and landed in front of us on his boney toes like a ballet dancer.

"Wait, which one of us is dead?" I asked, panicked.

"The man. Well, the god here, or the demi-god, or the whatever he is," the skeleton said as he motioned to Lontano, who responded by slamming his fist into the floor, repeatedly. As if that would do something.

"Whoa, whoa, whoa," the skeleton said as he waved his hand in the air toward Lontano. "Why are you playing the game if this makes you mad? This is how it works, ya know."

"I'm not playing of my own volition!" Lontano spat.

"Ah. Man, then this sucks for you," the skeleton said, playfully turning his hourglass back and forth in the air as he studied Lontano.

"How do I revert to my original form?" Lontano asked as he stood up.

"Well, I'll send you off to the cemetery. There's a monastery there where Friedrich lives. You complete a task for him, and then he'll show you where your body is buried. You dig it up and—*waalaa!*—back to normal," the skeleton explained.

"He was never normal," Hercules commented.

"Um, well. Either way, his spirit will once again be joined with his body," the skeleton said.

"If he's less of a threat as a ghost maybe we should just keep him this way," Nora suggested.

"My sister's soul is in that body. So we *will*

be retrieving it," Lontano announced. "Whether you three like it or not."

"I must admit, I think you guys are the most complicated group I've ever seen play this game. Good luck!" the skeleton said.

Then he snapped his fingers while yawning again.

And we were in an eerie *and* frightening, snow-covered cemetery full of broken, tilting tombstones. Bathed in cold moonlight, a haunting mist crawled toward us. A towering ruined monastery stood in the distance, and beyond that a dark, dense forest of leafless, twisting trees.

"*Ugggghhhhh*," Lontano groaned as he motioned for Ellie to walk to the monastery.

We trudged along a snowy path, through an archway in a fragmented wall, across a courtyard, and up to a massive set of frost-covered mahogany doors. Hercules deftly pushed them open with two fingertips.

Thank god it was warm inside, because we were certainly not dressed for standing around in a wintery landscape.

We found ourselves in a vaulted stone chapel, and next to the altar was an old-ish goateed man relaxing on a gold plush sofa, playing a match-3 jewel game on a tablet, and snacking from a bag of chips.

"You're not Friedrich," Lontano grumbled, his shoulders falling slightly.

"Too true, too true," the man answered. "Caspar had to tend to some business in a Whistler painting. He'll be back soon. I just stepped in for a moment to help him out with you guys."

"So what do we do now?" I asked.

"Yeah, I need to get my body back," Lontano added.

The man paused his game, brushed the chip dust from his goatee, sat up straight, and then stared us down.

"Named seven but I was truly six. I hid from riches, glory, and pomp. I began my time with ashen meat, stone seats, and a chamber of skulls in which to greet my guests. My coffin sat in my bedroom. 'Memento Mori' it sang out to me. But my mind was poisoned. The sanctity of life disappeared. I turned my stone seats into featherbeds, and the skulls into jewels. My thoughts about the inevitability of death turned into ambition. I filled my empty coffin with money as if that would halt death, and I could purchase life with riches," he said.

"Are you of sane mind?" Lontano inquired.

"By some I was painted as a villain. But was I really that bad?" the man asked. "Was I too greedy? What was I greedy for?"

"Whatever existential mid-death crisis you're having as a ghost is great and all, but can you tell me where my body is?" Lontano asked.

"I sensed someone special was coming to visit," the man said, smiling at Lontano. "Someone painted in greys."

"Are you going to help us or just continue this horrid Beat poetry reading?" Lontano asked, bitterly.

"Your skull is in a chamber Caspar and I have created *just* for you in a crypt beneath us. Find your skull and I'll tell you where your body is," the man instructed, as he pointed to a door on our left that—I guess—led to the crypt in question. "Let's see where your true skill lies, Tiziano."

The old dude's explanation was answered by an icy glare from Lontano, who was now biting his lower lip in frustration.

"I'm not going into a crypt," Ellie said, squirming.

"You have to. Or you can just do me the *grand*

favor of removing that following the leader spell and I will go down on my own," Lontano spat.

I shook my head at Ellie. It was too risky to remove the spell, or transfer it to Nora or my-self. We might mess up the most important spell —the one that made everything he did to us go right back onto himself. Sure, Nora had taken away the 'cry over spilled milk' spell without an issue, but time had passed. Our original spell might not be as strong as it once was.

Nora shook her head 'no' at Ellie, too. She rolled her eyes in response and sighed deeply.

"What did I ever do to deserve this?" she grum-bled as she stalked her way over to the doorway. "Hercules, you go first. Push any gross things out of our way."

Hercules scratched his forehead, and looked at her with a gaze that said, 'What did I ever do to deserve this?'

So she poked him above his belly button like she was powering up a microwave. He sighed, but turned and walked through the crypt door-way, swinging his club back and forth in front of him like a lazy pendulum, clearing the way of 'gross things.'

"Should we have asked that dude who he was?"

Nora pondered as we made our way down a set of steep, poorly lit stone stairs.

"The ghost of Fabio Chigi," Lontano replied.

"That actor model dude?" Nora asked. "I thought he was still alive."

"No. Pope Alexander VII," Lontano said, and then he sighed.

"Shouldn't ghost-Popes be doing something other than sitting around eating chips?" she asked.

"You'd think so," Lontano said. "But dying frees up a lot of your time."

"I guess it would," Nora said.

"You should try it sometime," Lontano said. "That is, if you can die."

He threw a sly, sinister smile at Nora.

"No one's managed to kill me yet," she replied with half-closed eyes and her nose in the air.

Obviously perturbed, Lontano mimicked her reply but without saying anything out loud, just with a scowling, scrunched up face. And Nora responded by mimicking his mimicking with a scrunched up face of her own.

"There's always the Godkiller," he suggested playfully, but he was clearly annoyed. "She could kill you."

"I suppose," she said. "I wonder if it hurts when a Godkiller kills you. *You* should try *that* sometime."

She grinned at him.

But a grave expression settled into Lontano's face, and he didn't respond. She studied his face for a split second, out of the corner of her eye.

"I once had this pimple underneath my chin and when I pressed on it, my left eyeball ached," she continued. "It was the weirdest feeling."

"Talking with you, you wingding, is the weirdest feeling," he said.

We had made our way down the stairs, down a long hallway, and down another set of stairs into a tunnel with a dirt floor and barely any lighting. Only the occasional lit torch hung from the walls.

Hercules was doing his best to keep gross things out of Ellie's way, shifting aside the detritus in our path with his club. So far this mostly consisted of spider webs. But as we got farther into the dark tunnel, broken bones, moldy pieces of cloth, mice (both dead and alive), mummified body parts, rats (both dead and alive), and large, unidentifiable very disgusting bugs were added to the list.

Luckily, Ellie's constant shrill squealing was muffled because she had her head buried into the edge of the lion skin that was hanging from Hercules' waist. He didn't seem to mind but the whole scenario really didn't give a lot of dignity to the front end of our adventuring group.

Lontano shook his head at her. Nora followed behind him, picking at her teeth with her pinky finger. And I made up the tail end of the pack, trying to keep an eye on everything at once, while simultaneously wondering why I was the last one in line.

Wasn't the farthest person back the first to get picked off by the zombies? Wait, were there zombies in here?

This thought made me cast a sensing spell to search for whatever had been hunting us. But it wasn't there anymore. Where had it gone? Had we left it back at the inn in Switzerland? Should I be happy about this or even more worried?

Just then we walked by a complete mummified corpse, where I regretted having eaten so much at brunch. And past that we found a coffin-shaped black door, covered in jewels. Hercules pushed on it with the end of his club. Several locked bolts popped apart, and the door came off its hinges, dropping onto the ground.

"That was probably supposed to be really difficult to open," Nora commented as she hopped on top of it and tried to pry off one of the jewels. "Get me one of these, Hercules."

We walked into the chamber. I assumed this was the crypt in question because it was full of skulls. It was easily two stories high, and larger than our whole house. There weren't any windows, but a channel of flames ran along a ledge in the center of the walls.

But back to the skulls.

Yes, there were skulls everywhere. Piles and piles and piles of them. It was one of those moments when you wonder how many there are of something. Like, 'Wow that's a lot of squished cars in that junkyard! I wonder how many cars there are?'

But then these weren't squished cars. These were skulls.

Probably thousands of them.

"Do you think these were all real people?" I asked, pointing to the piles.

"We're inside a Caspar David Friedrich painting. Nothing is really 'real' inside a painting. It's only 'real' according to that world," Lontano explained.

What the heck did he mean?

"So these were real people inside the world of this painting?" I asked.

"Yes. But they aren't really real people," Lontano answered.

*But what the heck did he mean?*

"It's best if you don't think about it too much," Hercules said, patting me gently on the head. Then he plucked a jewel off the door and handed it to a gleeful Nora.

Ellie had yet to detach herself from his lion skin kilt. And I don't think she had any intention of doing so given the fact that we were surrounded by a million gross skulls.

"How do we know which one is yours?" Nora asked, as she rubbed her earlobe.

"Uh. My teeth. I have perfect teeth," Lontano said.

And then he pulled his lips open and showed off his pearly whites to all of us. Well, those of us who were using our eyes at the moment.

He did indeed have perfect teeth.

I looked down at some of the skulls near my feet. They certainly did not have perfect teeth. Clearly this painting was from before the glorious dawn of modern orthodontia.

"I once brushed my teeth with maple syrup," Nora commented. "Just to see how that would go."

And then she started picking up skulls, looking at their teeth, and placing them aside. It took me more mental effort to make myself pick up the remains of dead people. But I girded my loins and eventually joined her efforts.

Meanwhile, Lontano was examining skulls left and right, tossing the rejects against the wall and shattering them. Such a considerate individual.

Hercules was occasionally rolling a skull over here and there to examine its teeth, but he was mostly just staring at the piles and piles of skulls in front of us.

"There's gotta be a better way," Hercules eventually said.

"Is there?" Nora asked, standing up.

"I don't know. But we'll be here until the end of time, so to speak, if we keep doing it like this," Hercules said.

"You said you could smell a gnat's fart on a windy day," Nora said to Lontano. "Can't you smell your own skull?"

"I don't believe I used those exact words when

describing my sense of smell," Lontano replied. "But no, I can't smell my own skull in here. I only smell a whole lot of death. It's kind of over-whelming to my nostrils at the moment. I can't *even* guess as to *why.*"

The King of Sarcasm, ladies and gentlemen.

"The Wynne brush!" Nora shouted, and then she pulled out the paintbrush in question from her pocket. "Let's use this somehow!"

"I have a better idea," Ellie interrupted her. "Lontano, do you still have your bloody towel from your nosebleed?"

"Yes," he replied.

"Give it to me."

"No."

"Do you want to find your skull?"

"Yes."

"Then give it to me, you stubborn rabbit turd," she commanded.

With an appalled look on his face, he produced the towel—which looked quite gross by now—from his bathrobe pocket, and waved it toward Ellie's head.

She uncovered her eyes to see the towel, but kept the rest of her face hidden. Was that really going to protect her from the gross things? Then she pinched the cleanest edge between the tips of her fingers and mumbled several spells underneath her breath, casting them onto the towel. From what I could hear there was a standard blood animation spell, and one of our unique idiom spells about needles and haystacks.

Then she let go of the towel. It dropped to the ground and everyone blinked at it.

"Is it going to explode?" Nora asked, clapping.

It didn't explode.

Instead it began to slink its way across the floor like an inchworm, crawling toward what I assumed would be Lontano's skull.

"Oh, thank god," Hercules said. "I didn't want to spend eternity in here."

"I never thought I'd be following a bloody washcloth to find a skull," I said, as we all walked slowly after the towel, watching its every move like we were taking our hamster for a walk or something. Although the towel was more the size of a guinea pig or chinchilla.

"I know, right? This just gets better and better," Nora said, and she smiled happily.

At least one of us was having a good time.

# CHAPTER EIGHTEEN.

*You And Me And the Ring of Secrecy.*

*By Stella.*

Archie was still seated on his mattress. Eating his blankets. The room was covered in orange powder and cheese balls.

Should I scoot closer to him? Offer hand holding again? Or just spend the night asking him questions the ring can help me get answers to? Hmmmm.

"Did Tezza say how long the ring's power lasts?" he asked quickly as I danced off into my thoughts.

"Hmmmm, did she? I don't know. How about I touch it to your hand again and we'll see if that turns it off?"

"But it could also just make the effect last even longer."

"Yes. That might happen."

*insert deep sigh from Archie*

He stared at me. I stared back.

"So you feel guilty about my Mom?"

"Yes. I mean, yes. Uh...."

"You shouldn't. I don't remember her. You can't miss what you don't know about. What happens happens, and people die all the time. Right?"

"Yes, but I was there right after it happened. And I was friends with Riot, or I thought we were friends, so I should've stopped her."

"You were there?"

"Yes."

"Do you know why I can't see her ghost even though a lot of the other people we are meeting seem to be ghosts?"

"Yes, I do. I sealed her body and soul into a special coffin and hid it in Old Kunkerpot's Realm so that Riot and Tiziano couldn't get to it. *Ack.*"

*insert another deep sigh from Archie*

"Can you take me there?"

"I can, with the help of the Four Dogs."

"Will you take me there?"

"If I can."

I looked down at my hands because I had started to tear up, unknowingly. Gosh. How can I be emotional about a woman I don't even remember? I stopped asking questions so that he wouldn't hear the probable tear-induced change in my voice. Then I sat up straight, coughed some, and looked over at him.

His eyes met my gaze, and then looked away, and then back at me. We stared at each other for just a little too long.

"Should I hug you?" I asked.

"Yes. I mean. Yes. I mean. *Unngghhh.*"

*Uuuuunnnnnnnnggghhhhhh.*

That one was my brain.

But nothing actually happened.

He seemed surprised at his own answer. And I was shocked at my ability to ask such an insane question. So we went to sleep. Or rather, we turned off the lights and lay as stiff as boards on our respective mattresses, under our own blankets.

I stopped asking him questions I probably didn't want to know the answers to.

And I think I finally managed to override Pu's spell. Either that or spell-brain realized what it would mean if this guy gave in to my bizarre flirtations: a brand new world of un-imagined imaginings. Perhaps faced with fear of the unknown, spell-brain too was overwhelmed.

I stared into the dark for a long time. I was happy that I wasn't being stupidly chatty. But I was also unable to fall asleep, lost in sad thoughts I wished would go away.

I must have eventually succumbed to sleep, though, because I had a dream about Lontano.

And not the kind of dream spell-brain would want to have.

He and I stood in an empty space. A black void with a barely-lit grey floor.

He was standing off in the distance, bouncing a rubber ball, catching it, and bouncing it again. All while staring at me.

Occasionally he took a few steps toward me.

Then a step backward.

All while bouncing that damn ball.

He was definitely getting closer, while pretending he wasn't intending to do so at all.

I couldn't move, which was unsettling to say the least.

Was this really happening? Had he invaded my mind instead of Archie's? Or was this just a buildup of my anxiety and stress releasing itself in an uncomfortable dream?

Then Lontano smiled and bounced the ball over to me.

I woke up, sat up, and looked around.

There was no Lontano. No ball. Just Archie and I.

I really needed to stop dreaming about this guy.

The next morning Pu returned from the shield without Medusa in tow. She had decided to stay behind to 'avoid the horrifically embarrassing atrocity' that is my life, Pu's words. But she also said that I could call her up anytime I needed her. So that was nice.

Raphael also returned, looking like he'd been dragged backwards through a hedge for hours in some sort of marathon catfight.

"Are you going to choose a task for us to accomplish now?" Archie asked him. "We need to keep playing the game to win it and get to the end."

"The sound of you screaming like a little baby when Medusa pushed down the fence at the hot spring is really enough of a gift to me. That will provide me with eternal mirth," Raphael replied, smiling at Archie. "Which is really all I've ever needed."

Raphael snapped his fingers and produced a small box. He tossed it to Archie.

"The key to my Palazzo Branconio dell' Aquila in the House of Coventry. It can be your love nest with Stella," he said, winking at Archie.

Then, still in our yukata, we were standing in front of an arched entrance to a huge hedge maze. An Italian villa stood behind us and ornate Mediterranean gardens in full bloom surrounded Pu, Archie, and myself.

There was no Raphael.

No Japanese bathhouse.

No goose.

No game board.

"Is it just me or did we miss a step there?" Pu pondered.

"Why didn't we go to the game board first?" I asked.

"It probably has something to do with Lontano's monster that's been trailing us since last night," Archie replied.

"What?" I asked. "*A what?*"

"Like one of those things you met at Penny's

old house in Pipistrelle Village when you touched the corpse dice," Archie explained. "It's following us."

"*Shouldn't we be more concerned about this?!*" I asked, panicked.

"Not yet," Archie replied, as he strode forward into the maze.

Pu and I followed him. He seemed to know exactly where he was going and this maze wasn't much of a challenge to him. Left, left, right. Forward. Right. Within a few minutes we were at the center of this hedge maze, where a gazebo was set up with a table full of food. An old man and an angry-looking woman were seated there, enjoying a luxurious meal.

"Archie!!!" the man said, standing up and shaking his hand. "Wonderful for you to join us. I hadn't remembered inviting you. Please sit down!"

So we joined the duo, and Pu and I began casually sampling everything on the table, pretending to be barely interested in the food, but still devotedly eating it, like polite guests.

"You're in the Game of Goose, and we're playing it. So do you have a task for us to accomplish?" Archie asked the old man.

"Am I? Are you?" the man replied.

"Yes, Titian, you are," Archie said.

"Well, you can get back my original Isabella d'Este portrait from this old cow who stole it from me last week and refuses to give it back. Says she doesn't want anybody seeing her as fat and old. But look at her, even as the ghost of a young woman, we all know Isabella gets fat and old."

The woman in question swore at Titian for a solid ten minutes.

"You're not getting the painting back," she said finally. "I've hidden it and plus, *we're not even in the Game of Goose.*"

"We aren't?" Titian asked.

"No, you senile old bat. We're at the Villa di Poggioreale in Naples in the House of Coventry, in 1493. Before Charles VIII invaded. This is where you spend your winter vacations, remember?"

"We're not in the Game of Goose?" Titian asked.

"No, we're at the actual villa. Not inside a painting of the villa, you moron. Can't you even tell? You're a blasted painter," the woman replied, clearly exasperated.

"*So we're not even in the game anymore?!?!*" Pu asked in shocked disbelief, tapenade falling from his mouth.

"*Gossshhhhdarnit!*" Archie said. "We were at a maze! So I thought we were still in it! I can't sense anything properly anymore thanks to that horrid Tiziano!!!"

"What did I do?" Titian asked.

Just then an eyeless monster composed of oozing black rubber peered at us from around the side of the hedge. It was standing on the same path we had just come from.

"Archie!" I said, grabbing his hand, and pointing to it.

I should've been super-concerned about the appearance of Lontano's super-creepy monster, but I had just touched Archie's hand and re-activated the spell. Like a no-brain ninny.

So all I was super-concerned about was holding hands with Archie and staring into his dreamy eyes. Like a no-brain ninny.

# CHAPTER NINETEEN.

*The End of Death.*

*By Morrow.*

The towel squirmed its way toward the back of the room, crawled halfway up a pile of skulls, and then disappeared underneath the jawline of someone who had not taken care of his teeth very well.

"That's not it!" Lontano scoffed, pointing at the skull.

"It's probably somewhere in this pile though," Hercules said.

So we started carefully removing all of the skulls to find where the towel's journey had ended.

We eventually spied it settled inside the eye

socket of a jeweled skull with perfect teeth. Lontano gleefully picked up his own skull and commanded Hercules to lead us back to the chapel so he could present it to Fabio.

When we got back to the gold sofa, someone else was seated on it, in addition to the ghost-Pope.

"Caspar," Lontano mumbled, nodding at him.

"Tiziano," the man replied.

Lontano sighed.

Obviously he had given up on correcting people about his new name.

The ghost-Pope looked impressed that we had managed to find the bejeweled skull so quickly, but not surprised.

"I guess you'll want to find your body now," Fabio said and smiled at Lontano.

"You think?" Lontano asked, scowling at him.

Caspar led us to a wall that was covered with inscribed plaques. He pointed at one that seemed to have been installed recently.

"Here lies the headless corpse of the worst person who ever lived," Ellie read it.

"Har. Har. Har. Har," Lontano fake-laughed.

Caspar grinned and tapped on the plaque. It popped open and a tray slid out with Lontano's headless corpse on it. Like at a morgue. Ellie turned away and started making dry-heaving noises.

Lontano placed his skull on the tray where his head should've been.

And his ghost disappeared.

His skull transformed into his normal head and his arms reached up, pulling it onto his neck. He sat up, looking pretty ticked off.

Fabio looked pleased with himself. And Caspar was definitely amused.

Lontano slid off the tray, slammed the drawer shut, ripped the plaque off with his bare hands, and proceeded to curse for several minutes while attempting to rip the plaque in half. But it was solid metal. He handed it to Hercules, who ripped it in half like it was a piece of paper.

"*This* is just not working for me. I might not be back for a while," Lontano announced, and then he dropped to the floor like a sack of potatoes, totally passed out.

"Did you kill him???" I asked Caspar and Fabio.

"No, he's not dead," Fabio replied.

"He just sent his mind elsewhere," Caspar added.

"How do we get it back?!" Ellie asked.

"Are you sure you want to?" Hercules asked.

"Well, what are we supposed to do now?" I asked. "Are we just going to be stuck inside this game forever with his limp body?!"

We all stood around limp Lontano, staring down at him, waiting for something to happen.

"Gosh, he's so handsome, even when he's passed out," Ellie said. "He needs to stop being evil and just be my boyfriend."

"Stop saying inappropriate stuff, Ellie," I said. "He's like a million years old and you're a child."

"I will mature," she insisted.

"Mentally? I doubt that," I replied.

# CHAPTER TWENTY.

*Bam! The Hedge!*

*As Presented by Stella.*

The monster hissed.

And then we were in a large grassy clearing on the edge of a forest of dry, spindly trees. Pu, Archie, and I were sitting on the ground in front of a large wooden door built into the side of a towering hedge wall.

And the monster was still with us. A goopy pile of black rubbery ribbons that lurched forward like walking, chewed bubblegum.

And then another one appeared.

And another.

*Was this monster mitosis or something?!?!*

If I had been of sound mind, I would've

been very concerned about the growing monster horde right next to us. But I wasn't of sound mind. Instead I slid myself closer to Archie and squeezed his hand.

And he didn't immediately stand up or scoot away from me.

Which was odd.

Instead he looked down into my eyes and smiled softly.

Oh, god.

That smile.

"*Isn't anyone going to fight those things?!?!*" Pu yelled, smacking the side of Archie's head.

Together Archie and I stood up to escape Pu's angry paw, but he didn't let go of my hand, and kept staring into my eyes.

More and more monsters appeared, encircling us, and crying out like they really, really wanted to eat us for dinner.

"What are you two doing?!?!" Pu shouted. "I know I wanted you two to act cute together, but this timing doesn't work for me."

"You're so beautiful," Archie said as he squeezed my hand.

Oh.

"If you honestly believe that, you must be

missing half your brain," I replied as I smiled back at him.

Yep, folks.

This wasn't Archie.

Son of a billy goat's crazy cousin. It was Lontano.

But I wasn't going to let him know that I knew he wasn't Archie.

Also, spell-brain was in it to win it. There was no way I was going to be able to override the recently reactivated spell.

We stepped closer together, and I wrapped my arms around his shoulders. He hugged me tightly, and gently rubbed his nose against mine. Then he went in for a kiss as I closed my eyes and slid my hand onto his neck, ring-down. He pressed his lips against mine as I squeezed his neck, and then I opened my eyes.

The creatures, just a few yards away from us, screamed bloody murder like crazed crows as they shot their black chewing gum arms toward us and enclosed us in a sphere of rubber.

Archie's eyes fluttered closed and then opened. Then he blinked hard as the screaming monster sphere fell away into piles of those squiggly, dusty little creatures.

And standing next to us was Lontano, twitching his nose at Archie in anger.

I was not about to be distracted by him, though. I kept up my kissing efforts like the crazed maniac I was, and Archie didn't stop me.

Amazingly enough.

Had I somehow transferred Pu's spell onto him?

*Was I dreaming?*

Was this really happening?

I noticed that the three Demington sisters were also here, standing next to an eight-foot sculpture of a mostly naked dude with a club.

Why would they be in a dream where I made out with Archie in front of Lontano?

Wait, why would I dream about making out with Archie in front of Lontano?!?!

Maybe I died and went to heaven? No. If I had died, I wouldn't have gone anywhere because I'm a Godkiller.

So this was really happening.

This was actually my first kiss.

And somehow it was with two men at once.

Somehow. That had happened.

# CHAPTER TWENTY-ONE.

*Bam! The Hedge!*

*As Presented by Morrow.*

We *had* been standing in the monastery chapel, talking with Caspar and Fabio about how to revive the seemingly comatose Lontano, who was still sprawled out on the floor, drool dribbling from his mouth.

But we weren't there anymore.

Instead we were in front of a door in the side of a massive hedge, in an entirely different place. Archie and Stella were several feet away from us, sucking face like their lives depended on it, wearing some fancy bathrobes.

Why was everyone wearing bathrobes now except for us?

Lontano stood next to them, pouting, and growing increasingly angry. Pu was on the other side, chanting, and cheering them on. An army of squiggly dust creatures surrounded us, but no one seemed to be paying any attention to them.

"I could watch this kiss forever," Ellie said.

"Me, too," Nora agreed. "Is that creepy? I feel like that's creepy."

"I'm pretty sure it's creepy that we're all standing here watching them like voyeuristic perverts," I said.

"*What are you two doing?!?*" Lontano whined, then tried to pry Archie and Stella apart. "She's mine!"

"She's not yours!" Archie yelled at him after he pulled himself away from Stella's face. "She's her own person."

Stella had yet to remove her arms from around Archie's neck and was going back toward his lips, while she ran her hand up the back of his neck, tousling his hair.

"I feel like a lot of stuff must've happened while we weren't around," Nora commented.

"Apparently! Apparently we missed out on the bodice-ripper part of this book," Ellie added. "This is incredibly disappointing to me."

I didn't know what bodice-ripper meant. I mean, I could guess, but I wasn't sure. But I *was* sure that we'd missed something, since the last time we saw Archie and Stella together they certainly weren't acting this way.

Meanwhile, Archie and Lontano were fighting over what Archie was trying to do by stealing Stella from him, yet again. Just like in L.A., using his sexual magnetism to draw her in.

"Alright, alright. I like her, okay? But I'm not taking advantage of my attractiveness. Well, maybe a little. But not in the way you're describing. Anyway, she's not mine. She's not yours. But I want her to be with me, not with you. I want her to be safe, and when she's with you she's not safe. So she has to stay with me," Archie explained his emotions in the most awkward way emotions were ever explained in the history of explaining emotions.

Lontano yelled something indecipherable and waved his hand toward the squiggly dust things.

They turned into hideous rubber monsters like the thing on the subway train, screamed in unison, and lunged toward Archie and Stella.

# CHAPTER
# TWENTY-TWO.

*The Rest of Everything.*

*By Stella Grum.*

"Bellerophon! Get rid of this guy and his monsters!" I commanded, tired of Archie being distracted from my lips, and scared of what those creatures might do to the girls. Although they did seem to have that giant sculptural bodyguard. So that was good.

Bellerophon appeared as Archie blinked and turned all of the monsters back into the harmless squiggles.

"What'd you say you want?" Bellerophon asked.

"Get rid of this guy and his monsters," I repeated.

Lontano turned all of the squiggles into monsters.

Archie turned them back into squiggles.

This pattern repeated itself about twenty more times.

The only one affected seemed to be Lontano, who had broken into a sweat and was beginning to have difficulty breathing.

"I think I'll have to take a nap," he said, now barely managing to remain standing.

"Every time you change those things back more and more of your power drains over to me," Archie said. "I am the God of this Realm, not you. So I'm automatically reclaiming what's rightfully mine."

"So should I get rid of him or not?" Bellerophon asked. "I think he might die on his own if he keeps doing this."

"He's killing himself," Archie replied. "If it makes you feel any better, Lontano, once you give back all of my powers you will be considerably less insane. Your demi-god mind was never able to handle them."

"Should I smack him over the head to speed up this process?" Bellerophon asked.

"Wait, wait," Lontano said as he lifted up his

hand in exhaustion and semi-surrender. "There's one thing. I haven't been able to change back into a skeleton since you came back into the House of Coventry and punched me. Before you kill me, let me get my sister's soul out of my body so Stella can try to save her."

"I don't think she can save her," Archie said.

"At least if she has the vial, she can try," Lontano replied.

"You can't turn into a skeleton while we're bonded," Archie said. "If you want to do that, you'll have to cut ties with me."

Were those instructions or commands?

Was Archie preventing him from turning back and using this as an ultimatum?

"You are a bastard," Lontano said.

I guess it was an ultimatum. When did Archie become so tough? Where was my shy, confused, fluffy bunny? Was this the effect of the ring of secrecy?

"It's your choice," Archie said sternly, staring him down.

He casually took his hands off my back and put them on his hips, as if to say 'I can destroy you even with both hands tied behind my back *and* this girl attached to me like a carbuncle on my buncle.'

Never mind about the fluffy bunny thing. Tough Archie was attractive as heck, too.

Lontano sat down, snapped his fingers, and produced a knife from thin air. He placed his left hand on the ground and stabbed it with ferocity.

Now there's something you don't see every day.

Then he snapped his fingers again, and the two porcelain figurines of my father and Penny with Eagle appeared on the ground in front of him, as well as a tin wind-up toy of a couple in a ballroom dancing pose.

Nora stepped toward them, but Archie held up his hand as if to say: Stop moving. So she did.

Lontano yanked the knife out of his hand, and pulled his bathrobe off his torso and arms. He took the knife and dragged it up his left arm, from the center of the first wound, slicing open his own limb all the way to his shoulder.

*Now there's something you really don't see every day.*

"I'm confused. Are we killing him or is he killing himself?" Bellerophon asked. "It looks like he's about to flay himself. Is that possible?"

Lontano transformed into the skeleton man as

273

he put the knife down on the ground. He reached into his ribcage and pulled the vials' chains off of his spine. He gently extracted them, chains clasped in his boney hand, vials softly clinking together. He carefully laid them on the ground in front of himself. And then he turned back into a man. He slumped forward and stopped moving.

"That's not dignified *at all*," Bellerophon said and clicked his tongue. "What kind of way to die is that? At least take a sword through the heart or something!"

I let go of Archie. *I must have been out of my damn mind!*

But I felt the need to check Lontano's injuries, which had disappeared by the time I knelt down. I covered him up with his bathrobe as much as possible, and shook him a bit, telling him to wake up. But he didn't. Archie knelt next to me, checking Lontano for a pulse, and trying to see if he was still breathing.

The Demingtons and the statue came closer. The girls looked confused and panicked.

"I really thought we were trying to kill him. Has the plan changed? Isn't this a good thing?" Bellerophon asked.

Pu slowly shook his head. I'm not sure if he was saying 'no' to Bellerophon's question, or because he was disappointed by me trying to help the crazy operatic clown.

Could have been both, or neither, really.

And then Archie, Lontano, Bellerophon, Pu, and I were no longer in front of the hedge. Instead we were on one of several dozen narrow staircases on the side of an underground wall, looking up at the sky, several stories above our heads.

Below us, about two feet down, was a pool of black water with flowerless, dark green lily pads floating on it.

"Where are we now?" I asked.

"An Indian stepwell. Destroyed, now in my Realm," Archie said as he stood up and looked around.

A different kind of plant, not a water lily, rose up out of the pool—roots, leaves, and all. It floated in the air in the center of the well, dripping water, slowly spinning. Then it began to glow, and just before it got too bright to look at, it transformed into a woman.

The woman and the air around her shuddered and one woman became two. The woman on the left side immediately became limp and dropped back down into the water. Face down. A floating corpse.

"*Ackggghhh*, Verbena," Pu said and tried to reach out toward the body.

He cast a spell and she began to slowly float over to our side of the well.

The other woman remained afloat in the air. She fussily smoothed and arranged her hair so it was neat and pushed behind her ears. She looked passively at Archie, then Bellerophon, then Pu, and finally Lontano and me.

I was still kneeling, holding him in my arms, pressing his head against my chest, with my hand under his jaw, searching for a pulse. But I was pretty confident he was dead.

"Is that the extent of it, Tiziano?" the woman asked. "Is that as far as your love for me goes? Lying there like a lump in another woman's arms after putting me in here?"

"Isn't him dying for you enough?" Archie asked.

"Did he really die for me?" she asked. "That sounds too full of loyalty and passion for someone like him. Anyway, he's not dead yet. Can't you tell? Oh right. You're not a God of Death like me, are you? But give me a moment and I'll take care of him."

The woman, who I had caught on was Riot, cast a powerful spell of some kind, which Archie casually blocked with his own magic, without moving a muscle. I think the extent of his effort was a blink.

"I see you're back to your old self," she remarked, glaring at him.

"Which means I can block you for eternity," Archie replied.

"That will get tiresome," she said.

While Archie didn't look concerned about standing here forever, I didn't want to be on these stairs for the rest of my life, holding Lontano's maybe-a-corpse.

"Bellerophon, kill her!" I demanded, pointing at Riot.

"Alright, alright. I got it," he said.

He snapped his fingers and Pegasus appeared in the air next to him. He jumped on his winged horsie, flew the twenty or so feet over to Riot, and smashed her over the head with his pointy stick.

She tried to block his attack, but only managed to get slightly injured arms, as well as a bruised skull.

But he didn't kill her. She wasn't dead.

Bellerophon flew back, jumped off of Pegasus, landed next to me, and snapped his fingers again. The winged horsie disappeared.

"I can't do it," he said.

"What? You're an icon. I'm the Godkiller. Don't icons kill for the Godkiller?" I asked.

"Yes. But *I* can't do it. You need somebody else with a particular skill. I've never done that kind of task. Well, I've killed gods before, but not a God of Death. Other types of gods. She's too powerful and I think her death needs to be a specific kind."

"You're the Force of Virtue," I whined. "This is a virtuous task. I assure you. You have to carry it out with your *force*."

"It's not me. It's gotta be somebody else," he replied.

"Well, what do we do now?" I asked.

"Call up Fortezza, she might know."

So I called up the Icon of Strength. And she recommended the Force of Love. And that angry Cupid recommended the Force of Justice instead. Who then recommended Castigo, the Icon of Chastisement. Who tried to cut Riot in half with his axe. But that didn't work. So he suggested we call upon Potesta, the Icon of Authority, to use her sword against Riot. Which also didn't work. Potesta mentioned the Icon of Defense Against Danger, who with her sword and hedgehog still didn't manage to get the job done.

Meanwhile Archie had cast a spell to keep Riot right where she was, which was good, because finding which icon could do what to whom looked like it was going to take awhile.

Soon enough there were more than two dozen icons milling about on all of the staircases, various animals and accessories accompanying them, everyone chatting and calling out to each other. All of them were trying to figure out who could kill this God of Death. Apparently none of them had done this particular type of task before.

So more and more icons were called, and I began to wonder if there was a maximum amount of icons my bracelet could call up.

Riot looked bored and unperturbed, mostly. But she occasionally shifted her arms outward, and rolled her shoulders as if she were uncomfortably sweating.

Then four columns rose up out of the well

water, one at each corner, and four dogs appeared on them, one dog per column. They were the talking dogs from Lontano's scary mansion in the woods. The dogs looked around at what must have appeared to be an icon conference cocktail party, sans cocktails.

"Is everyone having fun?!" one dog called out at the top of his lungs.

"Finally! You're here! Where have you guys been?!" Fortezza asked them. "This Jainkohiltzaile is clueless."

"Yes, we know. But we didn't know where she was until we sensed a massive gathering of icons suddenly forming at a stepwell in the House of Coventry," the furriest dog replied. "She's been hidden in the stupid Game of Goose."

"Tell her which icon can kill this God of Death so we can all go home, okay?" the angry Cupid said.

So the dogs explained how to call up the Icon of Divine and Humane Things in Conjunction. It's no wonder nobody suggested him because who would have even thought of that painfully lengthy and complicated name?

I did as they instructed and a kneeling man, dressed in light blue grandfatherly pajamas, appeared on an empty stair, his hands clasped together, and his eyes very, very confused.

"What's everybody doing?" he asked. "I was just about to go to sleep."

So the task we needed him to accomplish was explained, and Riot finally stopped glaring at Archie. Instead she looked down into the black water beneath her and sighed.

"We could work together," she said. "Me as a God of Death, and you as a Jainkohiltzaile who follows my orders. Then the Four Gods of the Apocalypse couldn't argue with that situation."

"Ah, so it was all down to them, huh?" Archie asked.

"It was their orders, with my own interpretation of execution," she answered.

I looked down at Lontano's motionless face. Was he really still alive? And then I looked over at Verbena's body, which Pu had hoisted out of the well with the aid of several icons. Drenched, disheveled, and definitely completely and totally dead. She looked to be only slightly older than I was. What had this girl done to deserve this fate? How could Riot even ask me to work with her—or rather *for* her? And I had thought Lontano was crazy.

"Man in his pajamas," I began. "Please do what I have asked you to do."

He nodded and lifted his right arm into the air, pointing to the center of the sky. A massive gold chain slid straight down from the clouds as if it were being pulled swiftly into place by an invisible hook underneath the water. It wrapped itself around Riot like a python.

Then the man in his pajamas forcefully clapped his hands together and opened them to reveal a tiny, burning star. He flung it at Riot's chest. It stuck there like a prickly seed pod, and slowly burned its way through her clothing, into her flesh.

"The chain melts her blood. The star will burn her flesh and destroy her bones completely. Now she will learn what it means to be a God of Death," he explained.

At first, she didn't scream.

She managed to pretend she wasn't in pain.

But then the screaming started. And the sound of it was enough to melt my own blood. To burn my own flesh. To destroy my own bones.

Archie was standing up straight, arms rigid at his sides. He was staring at her, and barely blinking.

I had to look away. Eventually I buried my face into Lontano's hair, and tried to plug my ears with my fingers. Pu came over to me and put his paw on my shoulder.

All of the icons and the four dogs watched in silence as Riot died.

After what felt like an eternity, the screaming stopped. And I looked up.

The chain still hung there. The star floated in the air. But there was nothing left of Riot. She was gone.

The man in his pajamas reached out his hands toward the star, which flew back to him, settled into his open hands, and disappeared as he pressed his palms together. Then he pointed once again at the sky and the chain was pulled back up into the clouds.

"Man must raise his mind to the gods," the pajama-ed man said to me. "He must appreciate their work and efforts. But the gods must also draw men into their own minds. They must appreciate the work and efforts of man. There must always be a cooperative balance. One side's agenda is never more important than the other side's. You should always remember that, Jainkohiltzaile. Also, I'm going to bed now."

And he was zapped back into my bracelet.

"Is anybody here good at healing demi-gods?" I called out to the other icons.

"You'd want the Icon of Health," Bellerophon replied. "Sanita."

So Sanita was called, a young woman holding a rooster under one arm, and clasping a viper-wrapped staff in the other hand. She was dressed in a physician's white coat with a stethoscope around her neck.

I didn't have to tell her what to do. She immediately sat down next to Lontano, picked up his wrist, and held it in her hand to read his pulse. Then she put her stethoscope onto his chest and listened. These standard actions were followed by more confusing ones.

The rooster had pooped on a nearby stair as it tutted around, and she scooped the poo up with her fingers and applied it to Lontano's palms. I gagged.

"Is that going to work somehow?!" I asked. "To bring him back from the brink of death?!"

"No, I just like smearing chicken poo on people," she remarked. "Of course it will help! My rooster has magic poop."

Then she motioned to the viper that he should

bite Lontano's arm. So he did.

And I looked at her like she was crazier than the man I was holding.

"It's magic venom," she said, noticing my shocked expression. "Calm down."

Next she peeled off a piece of the viper's skin that it had started to shed, and she placed it inside Lontano's mouth.

I was going to hurl. I wasn't even going to ask why she did that. I was just going to throw up.

Sanita touched the end of her staff to Lontano's chest and counted to eight out loud. The staff changed colors from white to black and then to red.

"Are you sure you want him to live?" she asked me.

I looked over at Archie, who shrugged in response.

So helpful. Although, the look on his face said that he was simply too conflicted to make this decision.

"He's just going to go back to being a Demi-God of Death, right? Nothing more powerful than that?" Pu asked Sanita.

"Yes, that's what he is now. He'll just be one that is awake and not in an expiring coma."

"Then fine, do it," Pu said.

She looked at me for confirmation.

If I didn't say yes I was essentially killing him as well as Riot.

"Save him," I said, nodding my head 'yes.'

I didn't need to kill two people in one day.

Sanita whispered something about needing to remember to pick up milk at the grocery store, removed the end of her staff from Lontano's chest, and he stirred in my arms.

His eyes opened and he automatically rubbed his face groggily, covering it in chicken poo.

"*Aaaaggghhhhhh, bleeeccckkk,*" he cried out.

Then he sat up and tried to use his bathrobe to wipe the poop off himself.

"That's the best part of this job," Sanita said and smiled at me.

Then the rooster, staff, viper, and Sanita were zapped back into my bracelet.

The other icons started discussing who wanted to go where for grilled eel, or a game night, or to watch an indie film, or attend a knitting club meeting, or whatever it was that was on their schedule. And they zapped back into my bracelet in groups, eventually leaving the stepwell mostly empty and quiet.

The last icon to leave was Bellerophon, who had waited until everyone else had left to nod at each of us knowingly. And then he was also gone.

The seven of us stood in silence, watching Lontano try to use the well water to wash rooster poop off his hands and face, while spitting out bits of snakeskin.

He eventually got to a point of either utter frustration or satisfaction at his level of cleanliness. He stood up and announced, defiantly, "I'd cast a spell to clean myself up, but I'm not strong enough yet after nearly *dying*."

Then he looked around the stepwell, probably noticing that Riot was not here, even though this is where he had put her. But he didn't say a word. His eyes glazed over a bit, though. So I think he knew what had happened.

Archie snapped his fingers and Lontano was instantly chicken-poo-and-snakeskin-less. His bathrobe was immaculate and perfectly arranged on his body as if he'd just slipped it on from the dryer. And all of his skin, which had been covered in dirt and mud and god knows what, was clean.

I also looked freshly pressed and cleaned.

Then Archie snapped his fingers again and the

eight of us were back in front of the door built into the side of the hedge.

Nora was holding the figurine of Penny and Eagle in her hand. Ellie had the wind-up toy in hers, and Morrow was gently poking the figurine of my father.

"If you had let me die, all of those things would have reverted back to their original forms," Lontano said, motioning to the figures.

"Or you could just change them back yourself," I said, as I picked up the chained vials from the ground. "You change them back, and I will ask every single icon if they can change your sister back. It might not work. But I will try."

He looked at me for a while.

I'm not sure if his facial expression was: 'You may have a good idea with that' or 'I'm really tired from almost dying.'

"*Rasori e pettini, lancette e forbici, al mio comando, tutto qui sta*," he began singing in a much less forceful voice than I had heard escape his lips.

My father's figurine floated out of Morrow's hands, up into the air, and in a poof of grey smoke it transformed back into my father.

"*Pronto prontissimo son come il fulmine: sono il*

288

*factotum della città,*" Lontano sang, and in an instant Penny and Eagle were standing in front of us.

Lontano then walked over to Ellie, reaching out his hand for the toy, which she hesitantly handed to him. He wound it up while singing something that sounded like a lullaby softly under his breath.

The toy couple began to dance in his hand and then it floated upward, dancing in the air, spinning, and whirling as Lontano sang to them.

And then there weren't any more floating toys.

Standing in front of us was a woman, a man in sunglasses, and a fuzzy baby cow.

Penny gasped and ran over to the woman, embracing her. She pointed to the Demington sisters and then dragged them over in front of this man, woman and cow. She chattered away, telling them their names and ages, hobbies, talents, likes and dislikes. All in between gasping sobs that were impossible to hold in. The man and woman knelt down on the ground in front of the girls and everyone hugged each other individually and then as one big group. These must be their parents.

My father looked at me, tears in his eyes, but he

didn't say or do anything. I expected him to run over to me and go off on a rant.

But he didn't. Instead he turned, and watched the ecstatic family reunion going on in front of us, a smile on his face.

"I notice you didn't bring something with us," Pu commented to Archie.

"I sent Verbena to rest in a coffin in Badger's Wood," Archie replied. "There was no need to bring her body here in front of the girls."

"There's a couple more things that need to be taken care of," one of the dogs spoke up in a bitter tone, while looking at Lontano.

Just then another man appeared in front of us, holding a screaming notebook in his hands.

"*Where's Sylvie?!?!*" he demanded, throwing the notebook at Lontano's face. "And where's Riot?!?!"

Lontano lifted his arm up and pointed at the door in the hedge.

"Sylvie's in there, but like Riot, I fear she's no longer with us," he said.

"Ozzie—this—Stella is the current Jainkohilt-zaile," Archie said, pointing to me.

"And she seems to have all of the powers," one of the dogs said.

"*Aaaaagggghhhhhh*," Ozzie screamed out, clutching at his hair.

He turned abruptly, ran over to the door, and tried to push it open. It wouldn't budge, so the huge statue man calmly stepped forward and smashed it apart with his club.

It splintered into a million tiny wooden pieces, which flew majestically into a room with morning-glory-vine-covered walls, decorated with several black paintings.

We all crowded in, one after the other, quickly looking each other over with sideways glances. Most of these people were definitely wondering what the heck was going on. I certainly didn't feel gifted because I knew what the heck was going on.

Inside the room was another woman's corpse, which Ozzie held in his arms and sobbed over.

I looked over at Archie. He was also crying, tears flowing down his face. He knelt down in his grief, unable to remain standing.

I quickly knelt down next to him, unsure of what to do.

Do I hug him?

I can't. The spell. I had just managed to override that.

I wanted to give him the warmest hug I would ever give. But how could I do that?

My father, whose face was already covered in tears, knelt down on the other side of Archie and hugged him. Yes, my father. Who I had never seen touch another man except for a brisk handshake.

Pu stepped up into Archie's lap, hugging him from the front.

I knelt there stiffly, my thoughts trying to arrange themselves.

What should I do?

And how should I do it?

The small mustard tin robot crawled out of Archie's pocket and walked over to Sylvie's body. He sat down next to Ozzie and the four dogs, and stared at her still face.

We were too late.

Everything before this moment felt so silly and stupid and pointless.

What could I have done?

Was there a way to have prevented this?

My chest felt empty.

My heart had collapsed into itself.

We were too late.

I watched Archie heave with sobs. I tried not

to start heaving with sobs myself.

I listened to Ozzie wailing over Sylvie.

I looked over at Lontano through my own tears. He was just staring sadly down at Sylvie's body.

Nora walked over to him, and took his hand.

And then he started sobbing even harder than Ozzie, collapsing onto the ground, with Nora kneeling down next to him. Morrow and Ellie joined her as Lontano cried out like his heart was being thrown into a fire.

I wanted to turn back time and do this all over in a way that wouldn't end here.

Not like this.

Never like this.

# CHAPTER TWENTY-THREE.

*Why You Should Write Things Down.*

*Written Down by Stella Grum.*

"*That's insane!*" my father huffed angrily at Pu, who had just explained how Archie and I are destined to be in love and together for the rest of my life.

Once that whole situation was said out loud, I realized how very, *very* stupid it sounded. And insane. Especially insane. And I also realized I wanted to crawl into a hole and die, just to avoid having this conversation.

"She's a sixteen-year-old high school student," my father continued. "There's nothing like that happening with her, for her, to her, around her, near her."

"They've already locked lips and there was... tousling," Pu commented, and made a kissy face.

The cat was clearly saying this to aggravate him.

And it was working, judging from my father's red face and locked jaw.

We were seated at the kitchen table of Penny's cottage, waiting to make our departure to Old Kunkerpot's Realm. There, in theory, I would meet the real, actual ghost of my mother.

Now that I thought more about it, Pu may have been explaining this whole Archie-love thing to my father in order to distract him from the fact that he would soon see his dead wife.

Was he doing that?

Nah.

That would count as kind and considerate, right?

That's just not Pu's style.

The oddest part of this scenario was that Lontano was also seated at the kitchen table, listening to this whole conversation, not saying anything, but looking like he really, really wanted to take a nap.

What were we supposed to do with him now?

I had the eight vials that had once rested inside of him around my neck. Yet he wasn't standing next to me, shaking me by the shoulders and screaming: "Fix my sister!!!"

Which is the type of behavior I had come to expect from him.

And then he'd try to pet my head or something.

"Is there an internet connection at this cottage?" he asked, his head leaning on his hand, after the conversation between Pu and my father had devolved into bickering about fake chocolate cupcakes.

"I assume so," I answered.

"And you have a room here?" he asked. "You live here with your father now?"

"No, no. We don't live here," my father interrupted him. "We live in L.A."

"Alright. So do you guys have an internet connection in L.A.?" Lontano asked.

"Why?" my father asked.

"I want to know if I have to set one up when I move in," Lontano said.

"*What?!?!*" my father spat. "You're *not* living with us!!!"

"Yes I am," Lontano said.

"No."

"Yes.

"No."

"Yes."

"No!"

"Would you rather I stalk your daughter for the rest of her life? Or just live with you?" Lontano asked. "She said she'd try to help me get my sister back. So I have to keep hanging out with her."

"Archie's going to have something to say about that!" my father replied.

"Ohh! Ohh!! So now you *finally* understand that Archie is destined to be with Stella!?!?!" Pu asked him, excitedly.

"No, no. I didn't say anything like that, I mean —I was just—the point is that you aren't living with us. We're going back to L.A. and living there *without you*," my father explained.

"Shouldn't you ask Jeanette what she thinks about all this before you, once again, make all of the decisions on your own?" Penny asked him as she entered the kitchen with Eagle, Tom, Naomi and the cow.

My father clicked his tongue.

"Good point! Or do you have something against listening to women?" Eagle asked him.

Just then Ellie popped out of a toaster she'd been hiding in.

"You can stay with us in my room," she offered to Lontano.

"*Noooo* he can't," Naomi interjected.

Archie and one of the four dogs appeared next to us—from thin air.

"That's so weird," Nora said as she emerged from a blender. "Having you just—bam!—show up. It's so weird here without Sven."

"Why are you hiding in our own kitchen?" Penny asked. "I told you girls to wait in your room."

"Everyone who wants to go to Old Kunk-erpot's Realm, raise their hand," the dog announced.

Morrow popped out of a coffee maker and raised her hand.

And everyone else followed her cue.

I was the last one to raise my arm.

Did I really want to go?

Archie, Pitkin, Ozzie, and the four dogs had gone back there already with Sylvie's body.

Ozzie was obviously still there. With Sylvie's

body. Probably still crying over it.

That wasn't exactly something I wanted to see again.

But my mother was also there.

Well, my mother's body.

And her ghost.

So I should meet her. Or something like that.

But I was so nervous that if someone suggested that I shouldn't meet her I would probably heartily agree.

I swallowed hard as the dog transported us all, with a deep sigh, to his backyard.

"Welcome to Old Kunkerpot's Realm. This will be Stella's home from now on," the dog said. "Ozzie's in the front yard with Sylvie's coffin. And your mother's coffin is in the gazebo. I'll show you the way. Also I'm saying this now to be *very* clear, we're not turning this place into a cemetery. No more coffins, people. Two is my limit."

"Oh, no. We aren't living here," my father said as he shook his head at the dog, who regarded the statement with a passive look of disinterest. Then he picked something from his teeth.

"Yes. Because everything you've done for your daughter so far has worked out *so well for her. So far*," another dog stated, in an incredibly sarcastic tone, as he joined us from the front yard.

"Wow," Pu said in awe. "It's like I don't even need to harass Derek if you guys are around. Wait, we should make a team."

"He's done just fine," Archie interrupted. "We can discuss all of that later. Let's go to the gazebo. Follow Muddiford."

I didn't want to follow Muddiford though.

I mean, I did want to follow him, because Archie was following him. Magnetic, magnetized Archie.

But I really didn't want to meet my mother.

I-yeesh-um.

Was there a way for me to suddenly transform into a really, really awesome and amazing person that she'd actually be proud of and happy to meet within the next five seconds????

"That's Stella," I said, pointing to Nora, while I looked at the ghost of my mother.

She had appeared out of the coffin once Archie pushed it open a little bit. She looked like a slightly older version of myself.

"I..." Nora said.

My mother smiled at me.

"That's definitely Stella," I continued, still

pointing at Nora. "She's cool and everything."

How far did I expect this to take me?

She just continued smiling at me, and then looked over at my father.

"Hello, Derek," she said.

He was already crying. So he grabbed Pu off the ground, and shoved his face into the cat, as a pathetic attempt to hide his tears. She stepped over to him and wrapped her arms around him.

"I missed you," she said.

"I...I lost him. I lost him," my father sobbed into Pu, who just hung limp in his hands, accepting his fate as a cat-handkerchief.

"It's okay," my mother whispered, squeezing him tighter. "These things happen."

But her voice choked up a little in the second sentence, and she started crying, too.

Lost who?

I looked over at Archie, with total bewilderment on my face.

Lost who?

Had I skipped over a vital section of these books by accident?

He answered my gaze with a quick head shake 'no' and half-smile-half-frown, i.e. the universal facial expression for: 'Not now. I'll tell you later when no one is around.'

So I looked over to Penny.

She also answered me with the universal facial expression for: 'Not now. I'll tell you later when no one is around.'

I sensed a massive conspiracy had taken place.

"C'mon girls, let's go inside," Naomi said to her daughters. "Lemmie and your Dad will make everyone dinner. I hear you girls are good at making desserts. Should we go make some?"

So the three Demingtons followed their parents and the cow into the house.

Lontano trailed behind them. Two of the four dogs followed him closely, and they strongly suggested that he should take this opportunity to change into something more than a bathrobe.

"Should I mention the fact that you guys don't even wear clothes?" he asked.

I turned back to watch my ghost-mother embrace my father and Pu.

It was just Archie, Penny, Eagle and myself.

I guess it was now obvious that *I* was actually Stella.

Not that it hadn't been obvious before. Nora looked nothing like a member of my family's gene pool.

Penny was also crying as she stepped forward to join the hug. Eagle contributed by hopping on top of my father's head and standing there majestically like a conquering emperor.

My mother smiled at Penny, Eagle and again at me.

Oh no.

I was going to have to join this hug, wasn't I?

Archie took a few steps closer to stand next to me.

Then he drew half of a heart shape in the dirt with his shoe. And looked at me with adorable puppy-dog eyes.

So I drew the other half of the heart with my shoe. And tried not to let my own heart explode from the cuteness.

Then he scooted his foot next to mine and gently pushed against it, as he nodded toward the group hug.

I get it. I get it.

So I joined the hug.

And started crying, too.

# THE (SORT OF) END

(Maple: Yay! You made it to the end of *Damaged and Diverting*! Are you still sane?? Probably not. I still love you though, even if you are now cray cray. Kisses.

Maple: Thank you so much for reading Maple's Fantastic Stories! The next part of Stella's adventure is currently being written by my magical dust bunnies. There is no set release schedule yet. But stay tuned, more is coming! I hope you will join us again in the future.

Maple: p.s. Baby bird farts. Sorry, I had to end this all on something really weird. Ta ta for now, friends. Stay safe and healthy.)

www.ingramcontent.com/pod-product-compliance
Lightning Source LLC
Chambersburg PA
CBHW021944170626
46808CB00001B/24